Born in Buncrana, Co. Done[...] English at Saint Patrick's Coll[...] at the University of Ulster, Coleraine, and at [...] Dublin. He lives in Dublin.

For the Abbey Theatre, Dublin, he has written *The Factory Girls*, *Baglady/Ladybag* and in 1985 the celebrated *Observe the Sons of Ulster Marching Towards the Somme*, which was presented at the Abbey and on tour. A new production (directed by Michael Attenborough) opened at Hampstead Theatre in London in July 1986. (This play has now won for Frank McGuinness the following: the *London Standard* Most Promising Playwright Award, an Arts Council bursary, the Rooney Prize for Irish Literature, the 1985 Harvey's Best Play Award, the Cheltenham Literary Prize, the Plays and Players Award 1986 (shared with Jim Cartwright) for Most Promising Playwright and the London Fringe Awards 1986 for Best Playwright New to the Fringe and Best Play.)

His play *Innocence* (on the life of Caravaggio) opened at the Gate Theatre, Dublin, in November 1986. Both *Sons of Ulster* and *Innocence* are published by Faber.

His new version of Lorca's *Yerma* was produced at the Abbey Theatre in May 1987 and a new version of Ibsen's *Rosmersholm* commissioned by the National Theatre opened in the same week. (His first film for television, *Scout*, was shown on BBC 2 in September 1987.)

Frank McGuinness will have two new plays opening in the 1988 Dublin Theatre Festival: *Carthaginians* at the Peacock Theatre and a new version of *Peer Gynt* at the Gate. He is currently working on a new stage play.

gal, Frank McGuinness lectures in
lege, Maynooth. He has also worked
University College.

CARTHAGINIANS
and
BAGLADY

FRANK McGUINNESS

faber and faber
LONDON · BOSTON

First published in 1988
by Faber and Faber
3 Queen Square London WC1N 3AU

Photoset by Wilmaset Birkenhead Wirral
Printed in Great Britain by
Richard Clay Bungay Suffolk

British Library Cataloguing in Publication Data
McGuinness, Frank
Carthaginians; and baglady.
I. Title
822'.914   PR6063.A234/
ISBN 0-571-15131-0

The publisher acknowledges with thanks
the financial assistance of
the Arts Council of Northern Ireland
in the publication of this volume.

CONTENTS

It is possible that there is no other memory
than the memory of wounds.

Czeslaw Milosz

CARTHAGINIANS

For Joe and Sarah

CHARACTERS

MAELA, in her forties
GRETA, in her thirties
SARAH, in her thirties
DIDO, in his twenties
HARK, in his thirties
PAUL, in his thirties
SEPH, in his twenties

SETTING

A burial ground.

The outline of a row of graves should be suggested, and the monuments, of which there should be a maximum of seven, should resemble in their shape and symbols those of the grave chambers found at Knowth.

Three plastic benders, of the type used by the women at Greenham Common, should be constructed.

A large pyramid, made from disposed objects, should be already near completion.

Carthaginians was first performed at the Peacock Theatre, Dublin, in September 1988. It was directed by Sarah Pia Anderson. This published script is the text of the first day in rehearsal.

SCENE ONE

*Monday morning. Music, 'When I am Dead and Laid in Earth',
Purcell's* Dido and Aeneas. *Light rises on the burial ground. Three
women sit in silence. As if dressing a young woman,* MAELA *spreads
clothes upon a grave.* SARAH *is sorting through a pile of leaves.*
GRETA *attends to a wounded bird.*

GRETA: Poor bird. Bad wing.

SARAH: I hope these are the right leaves.

MAELA: How can you have right or wrong leaves?

SARAH: Ask the expert. Greta has a way with birds.

MAELA: Show her what you have.

  (SARAH *takes a bundle of leaves to* GRETA, *who examines
  them and then places a few about the bird's box.*)

GRETA: You never can tell with birds.

SARAH: Tell what?

GRETA: Their nests, how they build it. You can learn about
  their flight and how they eat, but where they live, that's a
  mystery. Anyway, this boy won't live much longer. A
  goner. Poor old bird. God rest you. God rest us all.

MAELA: Don't say that.

GRETA: What?

MAELA: You only say that over the dead.

GRETA: We're all dying.

MAELA: No, we're not.

SARAH: Maybe not.

MAELA: Sarah, pet, you'll die of sunstroke if you don't take off
  that big jumper. Are you cold in this heat? Thank Christ
  for the good weather. How could we stick this place if it
  was raining? You see, isn't that a sign? Isn't God with us
  when he gives us this good weather? No matter what they
  say, what we saw – no, I'm wrong.

GRETA: What's wrong, Maela?

MAELA: Talking about it.

GRETA: About what, Maela?

MAELA: What I've seen.

GRETA: What the three of us have seen, Maela.

MAELA: If we talk about it, will it happen?

(*Silence.*)

SARAH: (*Sings, low:*) 'In the port of Amsterdam, There's a sailor who sings . . .'

(*Silence.*)

GRETA: Birds have a great way of knowing their own.

SARAH: How do they know their own?

GRETA: They sing.

SARAH: We sing as well.

GRETA: Then sing for me, Sarah.

MAELA: Greta, you sing. You have the voice.

GRETA: (*Sings:*) 'I have only one brother, may God rest his soul. He was drowned in the river.'

(*Silence.*)

Cheer me up.

SARAH: How?

GRETA: A joke, Sarah. A dirty joke. The dirtiest joke you know. We'll tell each other dirty jokes.

SARAH: A man goes into a doctor's office. He says, 'Doctor, doctor, I've got a pain.' 'Where?' says the doctor. 'Where's the pain?' 'Between my legs,' says your man. 'How?' says the doctor. 'It's fallen off,' your man says. 'What's fallen off?' '*It*'s fallen off.' 'Show me it,' says the doctor. Your man puts his hand into his pocket and hands it over. The doctor looks and says, 'That's a cigar butt.' 'Sorry, doctor, sorry. Here.' 'That's another cigar butt.' 'Here you go, doctor.' 'My good man, that is another cigar butt.' 'Jesus, doctor,' your man says, 'I've smoked it, I've smoked it.'

GRETA: Not bad, Sarah. You go, Maela.

MAELA: I know no dirty stories.

SARAH: Go on, Maela.

MAELA: The two of yous can tell the dirty stories. I'll listen.

SARAH: Go, Greta.

GRETA: Three women are sitting in a train. There's an

Englishwoman, a Frenchwoman and a Derry woman. Each
of them has a banana. The English one takes out her little
lunch-box and gets her banana.

(GRETA *peels an imaginary banana sideways. She giggles
girlishly and then eats it sideways. Delicately, she wipes her
mouth.*)

The Frenchwoman pulls her banana out from inside her
skirt.

(*Flamboyantly* GRETA *produces an imaginary banana and
devours it in two gulps.*)

The Derry woman has a brown paper bag.

(GRETA *reluctantly removes a banana from the bag. Raising
her eyes to heaven, she sighs. Wearily she peels the banana.
Seeing it naked she gazes at it with infinite boredom. Suddenly
GRETA grabs her own hair and repeatedly pulls her hair down
on the banana.*)

SARAH: That's the worst yet.

MAELA: I don't understand it but thank God we can laugh.

GRETA: Stops us crying.

(*Silence.*)

MAELA: Is he getting better?

GRETA: No.

SARAH: Poor bird.

MAELA: Will he die?

GRETA: Soon.

(SARAH *fingers the bird's head.*)

Leave him, Sarah. You bring him no peace.

(*Silence.*

MAELA *has returned to the grave she had been dressing and
speaks to it.*)

MAELA: You don't know the value of money, you know that? I
can't keep up with you. All you think about is style. Isn't
that right?

(*Silence.*)

GRETA: What age would she have been?

MAELA: You mean what age she is?

(*Silence.*)

Twenty-nine. She'll be twenty-nine this year, if God spares her. I'm saving for her birthday. (*Whispers:*) A leather jacket. I'm buying it for her. (*Raises her voice:*) But we'll see. We'll just have to see. Who knows?

(MAELA *sings. Silence.*)

'Happy birthday to you, happy birthday to you, happy birthday . . .'

(*Silence.*)

She's not dead, you know. She's not. That's why I saw what all three of us saw. That's why it's going to happen. It has to, hasn't it?

(*Silence.* DIDO *is heard singing offstage:*)

DIDO: 'But if you come and all the flowers are dying,
　　And I am dead, as dead I well may be – '

(DIDO *enters, pushing a battered pram, wearing a pair of Doc Marten boots, dyed pale blue, an 'Arm the Unemployed' T-shirt, and a long pink scarf.*)

　　'Oh seek the spot where I will be lying,
　　And kneel and say an Ave there for me.'

(*Silence. The women look at him.*)

Yes, heads, still here?

MAELA: Hello, Dido. How are you, son?

DIDO: Surviving, Maela. How are yous?

MAELA: Grand. Surviving.

SARAH: What's on your T-shirt, Dido?

(DIDO *displays his chest.*)

MAELA: 'Arm the Unemployed.'

DIDO: Solidarity, soul sister.

(DIDO *raises his fist.*)

MAELA: You never did a day's work in your life.

DIDO: It's the thought that counts.

GRETA: Where the hell were you?

DIDO: What do you mean, 'where the hell was I'?

GRETA: You were supposed to be here at ten o'clock. It's now half twelve. I ran out of fags an hour ago and Sarah's tongue is a mile long waiting for her coffee.

DIDO: Listen, wagon, I'm not running a charity service.

Business, baby, I've other commitments. Count yourself lucky I'm here. I had to fight my way to this graveyard through three army checkpoints. I could have been detained. There could have been an assault.

MAELA: What did they threaten to do to you, Dido?

DIDO: It was more what I threatened to do to them. No luck though. No score. I think they were on to me as a health hazard. One of them was nice. Blond. From Newcastle. Interested in football.

GRETA: How can you chat up Brits?

DIDO: Greta, you know my ambition in life is to corrupt every member of Her Majesty's forces serving in Northern Ireland.

GRETA: Jesus, that should be difficult.

DIDO: Mock on. It's my bit for the cause of Ireland's freedom. When the happy day of withdrawal comes, I'll be venerated as a national hero. They'll build a statue to me. I'm going to insist it's in the nude with a blue plaque in front of my balls. (*Holds an imaginary plaque before himself.*) This has been erected to the war effort of Dido Martin, patriot and poof.

GRETA: You dirty wee pervert, you –

DIDO: You're right, Greta. Give us a hug, Sarah. Prove my manhood.

SARAH: Give us the grub, Dido, or you're dead.

DIDO: Leave me in my sin. I ask for woman's love, I'm given –

GRETA: Give us the grub.

DIDO: All right, all right. (*Removes three flasks from the pram.*) Sarah, coffee with no milk and loads of sugar. Maela, tea with loads of milk and no sugar. Greta, tea with loads of piss.

GRETA: Thank you.

DIDO: Thank you. Maela, two ham sandwiches, mustard and some cheese. Sarah, cheese, apples, rolls, tomatoes, carrots, fruit juice, book.

SARAH: Book?

DIDO: A gift.

SARAH: Thanks, Dido. A hardback. Did it cost a fortune?

DIDO: Nicked it from the library.

GRETA: Where's my fags?

DIDO: Here. *Sporting Chronicle*, sixty Silk Cut, packet of chewing-gum.

MAELA: Are you on a diet? Only a packet of chewing gum?

GRETA: I'm giving up fags.

MAELA: Sixty Silk Cut?

GRETA: I'm cutting down. (*Inhales the cigarette.*) That's good.

MAELA: Nothing like tea.

GRETA: I meant the cigarette.

(GRETA *reads the* Sporting Chronicle. DIDO *takes more food from his bag.*)

I'm going to do you, young fella. The one o'clock at Edinburgh has a horse in it called Desert Orchid. I've been following its form all year. I miss it today because you're not here in time. If it wins your throat's cut.

DIDO: Where's the rare boy? Seph? Your ma sent this.

(SEPH *appears from behind a standing stone.* DIDO *gives* SEPH *his food.* SEPH *takes it in silence.*)

She says you wanted this as well. (*Takes a guitar from the pram.*) Guitar. What do you want a guitar for? Are you lonely?

(*Silence.*)

MAELA: This ham sandwich is lovely, Dido. Where did you get it?

DIDO: Made it myself. Cuts cost, Maela.

MAELA: That's very decent of you.

DIDO: For me, not you. That's no extra dough since you retired to the graveyard and the quiz team disbanded.

SARAH: Yous two have a quiz team?

DIDO: Yup, and a pretty good one.

MAELA: We were called Oldie and Goldie.

SARAH: How did you meet?

DIDO: Wandering the graveyard.

MAELA: We teamed up.

DIDO: Maela was dressing a grave.

MAELA: Dido was fasting to death.

DIDO: In protest. I'd been abandoned by this beautiful stranger. It was a form of suicide.

MAELA: He was looking for sponsorship.

DIDO: For the suicide.

GRETA: Sponsorship?

DIDO: Every little helps. Anyway, Maela talked me out of it. To pass the time we entered Derry City Super Quiz League and the money we won helped out my dole. But no more. So, what do yous owe me? Sarah, £1.40 plus my commission is £1.70. Maela, £2.00 plus my commission makes £2.50. Greta, £5.50 plus my commission, you owe me –

GRETA: £6.60.

DIDO: No flies on Greta.

GRETA: No flies on Dido either, but then he doesn't need them.

DIDO: Watch it.

(HARK *enters pushing a wheelbarrow full of clay. He is silent.*)
Hark?

(HARK *glares at* DIDO.)

I got you something to eat in case you were hungry. A few sandwiches. I hope you don't mind –

HARK: I have something to eat.

DIDO: I got you a few beers in case you got dry.

HARK: I'm never dry.

DIDO: You don't have to pay me for them.

HARK: I wasn't going to.

DIDO: Right, right, I see.

HARK: I'm glad you see. I'd be very glad if I didn't see you. I am sick seeing you. Why are you following me? I walk home at night and you are behind me. I walk out my door and you are in front of me. Jesus, when I'm locked in the lavatory, I expect to see you dancing under the door. You are known as a queer in this town. I do not like being seen with queers. I do not like queers. I do not like you. Fuck off.

(HARK *exits.*)

DIDO: I still say there's hope.

GRETA: Really?

DIDO: Definitely. He's just playing hard to get.

GRETA: Pretty successfully.

DIDO: Who asked for your opinion?

MAELA: Was anybody asking for us in the town?

DIDO: No, nobody. You're kinda stale news now.

MAELA: Us?

DIDO: You and your visions. Nobody believes them any more.

MAELA: They have no patience. No faith.

DIDO: They say they have more sense. They say only the
lunatics listen to you now. How the hell will the dead rise?

GRETA: Are you lunatic?

DIDO: No.

GRETA: Then why keep attending us?

DIDO: Business. I'm in this for the money. If you bring this
number off, you're going to be worth more than Our Lady
of Lourdes and Our Lady of Fatima rolled into one. I want
a slice of the action, I'm a devout Catholic.

SARAH: What's that got to do with it?

DIDO: Plenty. Your own kind think you're mad, but the Prods
think you're Martians.

MAELA: Who cares what anybody thinks, as long as we believe
in it?

DIDO: Exactly, Maela, you said it. Hi, Sarah, find any good
flowers for my collection?

(DIDO *produces an album of pressed flowers.*)

SARAH: No, I didn't go for my walkabout today.

(SEPH *rises and walks over to* DIDO. *He carries a plastic bag.
From it he empties on to the pram a pile of dead flowers. He
walks away from them.* DIDO *looks at the flowers, then at*
SEPH, *who has turned his back, then at* SARAH. DIDO *shrugs
his shoulders.* MAELA *has started to knit.*)

DIDO: Thank you.

(DIDO *starts to sort through the dead flowers.*)

MAELA: You must have a whole collection now.

DIDO: Yea, it's getting bigger.

MAELA: It's a nice hobby.

DIDO: Pressing flowers? Yes. Very butch. Very demanding, I haven't the time to press them all.

SARAH: Stop following Hark and you'll have the time.

DIDO: Oh, look.

GRETA: What?

DIDO: This was a rose, Greta. Isn't it beautiful?

GRETA: It's dead. I prefer them living. Why do you not?

DIDO: Flowers are more gentle when they're dead.

GRETA: Gentle?

DIDO: Yes. They have more power in them. More magic. You can work spells with dead flowers, did you know that?
(PAUL *enters hauling a black refuse sack, packed with rubbish.*)

PAUL: Pack of whores. Pack of queers. Pack of traitors. Look at the state of this town. (*Empties rubbish on to the ground beside the pyramid.*) Do you know who I blame for the state of this town? Do you know who I blame?

MAELA: St Malachy.

PAUL: St Malachy. He saw the end of the world. He prophesied it. He saw the waters rise over Derry. He saw the river Foyle and the Atlantic meet, and that will be Derry gone. He saw it, but will he stop it? No. He sees the state of this town, but so do I see it. And I will search every dump in this town for rubbish. I'm building a pyramid. When the dead rise, I'll walk into the pyramid with them and walk away from this town and the state it's in. And if I find St Malachy hiding in this city, I'll kill him, I'll kill him, I'll knock his teeth down his throat.
(PAUL *exits.*)

MAELA: Poor St Malachy.
(*She continues knitting.*)

SCENE TWO

Monday night. The women sleep. SEPH *sits, warming his hands
before the remains of a fire. He withdraws to the shadows.* PAUL
*enters, steadier on his feet. He goes to the rubbish abandoned earlier
and starts to add to the pyramid. He soon leaves it. In silence he
walks about the sleeping women.*

GRETA: The bird's dead. The blackbird. I couldn't save it.

PAUL: Who wrote *Tristram Shandy*?

GRETA: Black.

PAUL: An Irishman wrote it. That's your only clue.

GRETA: It couldn't fly and it wanted the air. It needed wings.
The wings weren't there.

PAUL: Lawrence Sterne wrote *Tristram Shandy*. Nobody's read
it in this town. Maybe two or three. Why was the bird
black?

GRETA: Paul, how do I know?

PAUL: You know everything about birds. Didn't they give you
the sign?

GRETA: If they did, I don't believe in signs any more. It died.
The bird died. It died from cold. It was black because it
was cold.

PAUL: Go to sleep, Greta.

GRETA: (*Sings:*) 'I had only one brother, may God rest his soul.
He was drowned in the river – he was drowned in the
river – '
(*Silence.*)

PAUL: Do you want to talk?

GRETA: No.

PAUL: Do you want to sing?
(*Silence.* PAUL *kneels beside* GRETA.)
I was at a quiz tonight, but I said nothing. I used to run it.
Questions and answers. What's the capital – ? Who won an
Oscar for – ? Who captained Arsenal – ? Fuck sports

questions. Selling out. Who wrote *The Aeneid*? Virgil. Who
did Virgil guide through the city of hell? That's a tough
one, boys. Who will guide me through this city of hell?

GRETA: Do you not guide yourself?

PAUL: Through Derry? It's grown foreign to me, Derry.

GRETA: How's it foreign? Weren't you born in it?

PAUL: Because I'll die in it. That's how it's foreign, this town.

GRETA: It's only a town.

PAUL: A port of sizeable population.

GRETA: It's only home.

PAUL: A harbour. An empire. Part of a great empire.

GRETA: British Empire?

PAUL: That's dead. Roman Empire.

GRETA: Catholic?

PAUL: Roman. This city is not Rome, but it has been destroyed
by Rome. What city did Rome destroy?

GRETA: Carthage.

PAUL: Correct. Two points. Carthage.

GRETA: How are we in Carthage?

PAUL: Tell them you saw me sitting in the ruins, in the
graveyard. I live in Carthage among the Carthaginians,
saying Carthage must be destroyed, or else – or else –

GRETA: What?

PAUL: I will be destroyed.
(*Silence.*)
I would like to go to Carthage.

GRETA: I would like to go to Rome.

PAUL: I would like to see the pyramids. I'm building a
pyramid. But I'm no slave. I am Carthaginian. This earth is
mine, not Britain's, nor Rome's. Mine. Am I right?
(*Silence.*)
Am I right?
(*Silence.*)
Are you asleep?
(*Silence.*)
Good. Who wrote *The Aeneid*? An Irishman wrote it.
That's your only clue.

(*Silence.*)

Do you give up?

(HARK *appears.*)

HARK: Virgil.

PAUL: Correct. Good night.

HARK: Where are you going?

PAUL: Here.

HARK: Where else is for you?

PAUL: Here.

HARK: That's not an answer.

PAUL: That's not a question.

HARK: So what's a question?

PAUL: Will the dead rise?

HARK: Yes.

PAUL: What makes you so sure?

HARK: Aren't the living here?

PAUL: Sometimes.

HARK: The women never leave.

PAUL: They're women.

HARK: Better than men?

PAUL: Who?

HARK: Women?

PAUL: Women.

HARK: Women.

PAUL: Who wrote *Tristram Shandy*?

HARK: Lawrence Sterne. He was an Irishman.

PAUL: That's your only clue. I never read it.

HARK: It's shite.

PAUL: Good night.

(PAUL *lies down and sleeps near* GRETA. HARK *stands alone, looks about the women. Silence.*)

HARK: Well, here they all are. The lunatics. Have they seen a holy thing? They believe in miracles. What are we going to do with them? Mad. Mad as March hares. Lovely way of putting it. Mad. Poor Paul. Poor – poor who? Nobody's poor, son, if you have your health. All the money in the world, but without your health, nothing. I'm sounding like

— who am I sounding like? I'm sounding like myself.
Myself, myself, myself —
(DIDO *enters*.)

DIDO: Are you all right, Hark?

HARK: How long have you been here?

DIDO: Not long.
(*Silence*.)
Why did you insult me today?

HARK: Because you deserved it.

DIDO: What makes you think that?

HARK: Why are you here?

DIDO: Want to be with you.

HARK: I hate you.

DIDO: You're with me. Why?
(*Silence*.)

DIDO: I don't like myself much either.

HARK: Well, I'm working on it.
(*Silence*.)
You're a woman.

DIDO: Do you want a cigarette?

HARK: You don't smoke, Dido. Why do you offer me a
cigarette?

DIDO: I smoke sometimes.

HARK: When other people run out, you smoke. Fags in the
packet to win them over. What do you want, Dido?

DIDO: To go home.

HARK: Where's home?

DIDO: Here in Derry, I suppose.

HARK: Derry.

DIDO: Come home, Hark. I'll walk you there.
(*Silence*.)
Are you all right, Hark?

HARK: Are you all right, Dido?

DIDO: No.

HARK: Good. You shouldn't be. Have you ever been picked up,
Dido?

DIDO: Not as much as I'd like to be. Come on, Hark, we'll —

(*Silence.*)

HARK: Picked up, Dido. Will I pick you up? Isn't that what you
want? Do you not want me? Do you want me, Dido?

DIDO: Not at the minute.

HARK: Don't be fussy. Will I show you how to pick someone
up? This is how, Dido.

(HARK *beats* DIDO *about the face.*)

And after that, Dido, do you know what they do?

(HARK *caresses* DIDO's *groin.*)

Does it not turn you on? Answer to your wildest dreams?
Me, Dido.

DIDO: Leave me alone.

(HARK *beats* DIDO's *face again.*)

HARK: Tell me the truth. Tell me who you're involved with.
Give me names, Harkin. Give me addresses. Just names
and addresses. That's all we're looking for. You can walk
out of here if you just give me one name and address. Tell
me.

DIDO: Hark.

HARK: Who's Hark? Tell me, who's Hark? Is he your
boyfriend? Do you love him? Is he a married man? Would
his wife like to hear about it? Would his girlfriend? Who's
she? Tell me.

DIDO: Let me go.

HARK: I'll let you go if you tell me. Tell me what's between
your legs. Is there anything between your legs? Is there one
between your legs? Is the united Ireland between your legs?
What happens when cocks unite? Disease, boy, disease.
The united Ireland's your disease. Does your cock want a
united Ireland? Will it tell me? Would you like it to tell
me? Tell me your disease. Tell me. Tell me.

SEPH: Tell him. Tell. I'll tell.

(*Silence.* HARK *releases* DIDO. DIDO *spits at* SEPH. SEPH
retreats to the shadows. HARK *sits.*)

HARK: Bad, bad, bad, bad, bad.

(*Silence.*)

Now you know. Will you leave me alone now? Do you

know my kind now?

DIDO: I know my kind, Hark. Do you want me to name them? Well, there's me. That's all. That's enough. I know how to use what's between my legs because it's mine. Can you say the same? Some people here fuck with a bullet and the rest fuck with a Bible, but I belong to neither, so I'm off to where I belong. My bed. On my own. My sweet own.

(DIDO *exits*.)

HARK: On your own.

(*Silence.*)

Fuck off, Dido.

(*Silence.*)

Fuck off, Hark.

(*Silence.*)

SARAH: Hark?

HARK: No.

SARAH: What have you done?

HARK: What I had to do. It was good for him. Wise him up.

SARAH: We need him.

HARK: I don't.

SARAH: He's a good kid.

HARK: There's been better lost.

SARAH: Johnny?

HARK: Don't call me Johnny. I used to be called that. But I'm not any more. Johnny is dead now and only Harkin remains. That's all that's left. The rest is dead.

SARAH: No, he's still inside.

HARK: Where he belongs.

SARAH: Come on, come here.

HARK: No. Take a pill, Sarah. Take a powder. Make yourself happy. Forget me. But be careful. You can get hooked on things like that. And you know what hooks do. They tear you. They bleed you. And they can bleed all around you.

SARAH: I'm clean, Hark. I've been clean for a while. Do you not believe –

HARK: I've believed you before.

(*Silence.*)

(*Sings:*) 'In the port of Amsterdam, there's a sailor who
sings . . .'
(*Silence.*)
Sarah.

SARAH: What?

(HARK *lifts up the dead bird.*)

HARK: The poor bird.

SARAH: What about it?

HARK: It's dead.

SARAH: Did you kill it?

HARK: No.

SARAH: Well, it's not your fault then, is it?

(HARK *walks towards* SARAH. *She takes him within her
blanket. They lie together.* SEPH *reappears from the shadows.
He watches them in silence.* MAELA *rises from sleep. She
carries a blanket to the grave she dresses and speaks to it.*)

MAELA: It's cold tonight.

(*Silence.* MAELA *sees* SEPH.)

Isn't it cold? Don't you find it cold?
(*Silence.*)
My daughter's in there. She's waiting for us. Who do you
have belonging to you dead?
(*Silence.*)
Well, good night. I'll see you in the morning. Do you think
it will happen? Will the dead rise?
(*Silence.*)
Tell me a joke.
(*Silence.*)
Will I tell you one? A woman walks into the doctor's office
and she says, 'Doctor, doctor, I've a pain.' 'Where's the
pain?' says the doctor. The woman says, 'In my child, in
my child there is a pain. A pain in her heart and in her
head and in her hair.' They call the pain cancer. So the
doctors shave the child bald and the child dies with no hair.
Isn't that a great joke? Isn't it?

22

SCENE THREE

PAUL *continues to construct the pyramid.* MAELA *knits the jumper.*
HARK *and* SARAH *play chess.* SEPH *watches them play.* GRETA *sits apart.*

HARK: (*Sings low:*) 'The Flintstones, meet the Flintstones,
    They're a modern stone-age family.
    From the town of Bedrock,
    They're a page right out of history.'
  Paul, do you remember *The Flintstones*?
PAUL: 'Let's ride with the family down the street,
    Through the courtesy of Fred's two feet.'
HARK: 'When you're with the Flintstones – '
PAUL: 'Have a yabba-dabba-dooh time.'
HARK: 'A dabba-dooh time.'
PAUL and HARK: 'We'll have a gay old time.'
PAUL: 'Maybe someday Fred will win the fight.'
HARK: 'Then that cat will stay out for the night.'
PAUL and HARK: 'When you're with the Flintstones,
    Have a yabba-dabba-dooh time, a dabba-dooh,
    We'll have a gay old time.'
MAELA: God, aren't men right eejits?
HARK: Hit me with a question, maestro, any question
  concerning *The Flintstones*.
PAUL: Fred's favourite food?
HARK: Brontosaurus steak and cactus juice.
PAUL: What lodge did they belong to?
HARK: Water Buffalo.
PAUL: Full title, please?
HARK: What?
PAUL: Loyal Order of Water Buffalo.
HARK: Jesus, were Fred and Barnie Loyalists? Orange Water
  Buffalo men?
  (HARK *howls.*)

SARAH: Your move, Johnny.

(HARK *ponders on the chess board.*)

MAELA: Have you buried the bird yet?

GRETA: I should have put it out of its misery.

MAELA: How was it misery?

GRETA: It couldn't fly.

MAELA: It could feel. It could feel you looking after it. I'd say it had a happy death. (*Nods significantly at* HARK *and* SARAH *to* GRETA *and whispers:*) Poor Dido will be heartbroken.

GRETA: Where is he today?

MAELA: Maybe he's sick.

GRETA: He'll feel my tongue when he strolls in.

MAELA: You were very good to get us stuff, Hark.

HARK: I'm playing chess, Maela. Shut up.

(PAUL *holds up various pieces of rubbish, then arranges them into the pyramids.*)

PAUL: Am I mad?

(*Silence.*)

Sometimes am I mad?

MAELA: You're definitely not well all the time, son. And you catch anything handling that rubbish.

PAUL: It's not rubbish. It's precious. It's stone for the pyramid. Pharaohs constructed pyramids with the hands of slaves. I am not a slave. I construct with my own hands.

GRETA: Why on under God are you building a pyramid?

PAUL: My pyramid, my monument, my hands. My hands, my hands. Am I right, Harkin? Am I right?

HARK: You've got a point there, Paul. Point there. (*Moves a chess piece.*) Get out of that one, girl.

(SARAH *moves abruptly.*)

HARK: Shit.

PAUL: I won't give up. I'll build on. Everything has to be exact. Every measurement. Through here the dead will find their way back to this world. When I'll finish, they'll rise, the dead. So I'll keep going.

MAELA: That's the boy, Paul. Keep going.

GRETA: You're as bad as he is.

MAELA: Maybe so.

SARAH: What are you knitting?

MAELA: A jumper. It'll soon be getting colder at nights.

SARAH: That looks good and thick. It should warm you.

MAELA: It's not for me. It's for her. She loves pink. It suits her.

HARK: She's dead, Maela. She's in the grave.

MAELA: Maybe to some, not to me.

HARK: You buried her, Maela.

MAELA: There was nothing in the coffin. She's not dead.

HARK: She is. They all are, women. They won't rise.

MAELA: Stop him talking like that, Sarah.

HARK: The dead don't rise. I know. I put them in the earth. Once they go in there, they're swallowed up for ever and ever amen. So be it. Let them rest, girls. Give up your vision. The dead won't rise in Derry graveyard. Go home.

MAELA: Sarah, shut up that hateful bugger.

SARAH: Move, Hark.

(HARK *moves a chess piece.* SARAH *immediately counter-attacks.*)

Checkmate.

HARK: The king is dead.

SARAH: Long live the king.

HARK: God save the king. God save the queen. My favourite song. Morning, noon and night I sing it.

MAELA: Gaol affected your mind.

HARK: My mind. Everybody's mind.

PAUL: I know what I'm doing this time. I have to follow the shape of the stars. They're telling me something.

GRETA: They're telling you nothing.

PAUL: I have to have faith in something.

GRETA: Have faith in yourself.

PAUL: Do you?

GRETA: I'm too tired to have faith.

(HARK *leaps to his feet.*)

HARK: Do I hear the cry of a lost soul? Why, my daughter, have you abandoned hope? Why do you turn your back on the faith of your childhood?

25

GRETA: I blame it on television myself.

HARK: Christ, Greta, you're smart.

GRETA: Think so?

HARK: A walking monument to the wit and wisdom of Derry town.

GRETA: Dear lovely Derry.

HARK: Dear drunken Derry, where even the women are too pissed to get it up.

GRETA: The wit and wisdom of Derry town.

HARK: Through wit and wisdom we shall overcome. (*Sings:*) 'We shall overcome.'

GRETA: 'We shall overcome.'

HARK: 'We shall overcome.'

GRETA: 'We shall overcome.'

HARK: 'We shall overcome someday.'

GRETA: 'Deep in my heart I do believe.'

HARK: 'We shall overcome someday.'

GRETA: 'We'll walk hand in hand.'

HARK: 'We'll walk hand in hand.'

MAELA: 'We'll walk hand in hand someday.
    For deep in my heart I do believe.
    We shall overcome someday.
    We are not alone.'

SARAH: 'We are not alone.
    We are not alone today.'

MAELA: 'For deep in my heart I do believe.'

PAUL: 'We shall overcome.'

HARK: 'Someday.' (*Affects an American accent:*) Brothers and sisters, I have a dream.

GRETA: What is your dream, brother?

HARK: That someday we shall be one. One people, one nation, one country. Black and white, white and black, sisters and brothers, brothers and sisters. Catholics shall stand with Catholics, Protestants with Protestants –

MAELA: Should it not be 'Catholics will stand with Protestants'?

HARK: I speak of dreams, sister, not of insanity. Let us be like the asshole and let us be apart. Let us live apart as we

26

choose to live apart. Let us hate as we wish to hate. Let us
wander forth into the wilderness of bigotry and let us
spread more bigotry. Let us create a nation fit for assholes
to live in, for as assholes are we known to each other and
like the asshole let us for ever remain apart.

(DIDO *enters, pushing the pram, dressed in football gear.*)
Hello, Dido. What kept you? Have they changed the
visiting hours? Were you strip-searched. Did you enjoy
that? Have you brought me something nice? Books,
comics, clothes, change of socks, shirts, underwear? Did
you bring me underwear, Dido? Why have you brought me
nothing, Dido? Do you not love me? Am I a shite? Am I a
fucker? Am I sorry?

(*During this* DIDO *has stood, silent and unmoved. He then
reaches into the pram and produces a long string of sausages.
He juggles expertly with the sausages, then walks to* HARK.)

DIDO: Pick a sausage, any sausage.

(HARK *points to a sausage.* DIDO *continues to juggle with the
sausages, then gathers them together, opens* HARK's *shirt, crams
the sausages into the shirt, batters his fists against* HARK's *shirt,
takes out the resultant mess, points to it.*)

Is this your sausage? Then have it.

(DIDO *flattens the sausages into* HARK's *face, rubbing the meat
in vigorously.*)

MAELA: That wasn't very nice, Dido.

DIDO: You're right, Maela. I should make it up to him.

HARK: Don't touch me.

DIDO: Nonsense. I simply insist.

(DIDO *removes* HARK's *shirt and throws it to* SARAH.)

You wash, and I'll dry.

(*From the pram* DIDO *produces a towel, a basin and a flask of
hot water.*)

The things I do for you even if I've lost you.

SARAH: So you know?

DIDO: Everything. I made inquiries. Don't worry. I've got over
worse.

(DIDO *has started to clean* HARK's *chest.*)

27

Alone again. Alone and powerful. Jesus, I wish I could meet somebody. Somebody rich. I need money. Big money. Look at me.

GRETA: What are you doing in your knickers?

DIDO: Passing the time. What do you do in yours?

GRETA: Wait for a miracle.

DIDO: Seriously, these togs are about the best stitch I possess. How am I ever going to make it dressed like I do? I need clothes. I really need a leather jacket. Leather. I need leather.

MAELA: Why leather?

DIDO: Sado-masochism. That's where his future lies, sado-masochism.

MAELA: What's that?

DIDO: You fancy somebody, you take them to bed, you beat shite out of them.

MAELA: I see. Marriage.

DIDO: Not exactly. There's pleasure in sado-masochism.
(DIDO *tweaks* HARK's *nipple.* HARK *yelps.*)
Just practising. Shirt?
(DIDO *fetches* HARK *a shirt from the pram.*)

MAELA: Think of the happiest day of your life and you won't need money.

GRETA: The happiest day of my life I made money. I backed the Derby winner for the first time. Secreto was the horse's name. It survived an objection. It won. Good old Secreto.
(DIDO *has started to clean* HARK's *face.*)

DIDO: The happiest day of my life is a secret.

SARAH: What happened?

DIDO: All right, I'll tell you. I was so happy I thought I was dreaming. I probably was for there was a man involved. He was foreign and he was pissed but he was beautiful. I met him when I was wandering the docks.

MAELA: Was he a sailor?

DIDO: Likely. I didn't ask. He came up to me carrying red roses and he gave them to me. He said his name was John. He told me he was from Lebanon.

(*With his hand* DIDO *gently washes* HARK's *face.*)

MAELA: What was he doing in Derry?

DIDO: Wandering through, like myself. When he give me the flowers I was sure I'd scored and then he put his hand to my face and I thought yippee but he just knelt down on the ground like this. (*Kneels.*) He said, 'Listen, listen to the earth. The earth can speak. It says, "Cease, cease your violent hand, for I am the earth and I accept my dead but I will no longer accept your dead, given to me by your violent hand. I am a peaceful earth, give me not your dead." '

(DIDO *rises and towels* HARK's *face dry.*)

Then he turned really weird.

SARAH: How? What did he say?

DIDO: 'The earth has a dream, and I pray my dream comes true.' I said, 'I pray your dream comes true as well but failing that I'll settle for Derry City winning the European Cup.' He smiled and called me Dido. I'd never met him or any like him before. It was as if he knew me. I turned on my heel and ran like hell.

MAELA: What about the flowers?

DIDO: The roses? They died.

HARK: They never will.

DIDO: They always do, flowers.

HARK: No, Derry City will never win the European Cup.

DIDO: Never underestimate.

HARK: How long will it take?

DIDO: How soon?

HARK: God knows.

DIDO: Need to build up a good team. Local. Loyal.

HARK: You need money. Only money talks.

DIDO: Yea, I need money.

SARAH: Then make it.

DIDO: How?

(SARAH *raises the king and queen chess pieces.*)

SARAH: Buying, selling.

DIDO: What are you talking about?

SARAH: A story. A story of buying and selling. That's how to make money, Dido.

DIDO: Telling stories?

SARAH: You do that.

DIDO: I might.

SARAH: I did the buying and selling. No deal without money. No money without dream. I had a dream. My veins were full of money. I felt a rich woman. I had my fill of money. I bought it myself and I sold it. 'In the port of Amsterdam there's a sailor who sings – '

(SARAH *lets the queen fall*.)

HARK: What does he sing about?

SARAH: He sings and he sings to the whores of Amsterdam who have promised their love to a thousand other men. (*Lets the king fall*.) Have you ever seen the Alps, Dido? They're white like powder. My fingers moved like needles about the Alps. Touch myself. Jag myself. (*Removes the heavy jumper, wearing beneath it a T-shirt, showing her bare arms*.) I walked by the canals of Amsterdam. I was sinking under the weight of money. I sank and I sank until I felt hands lift me. I thought they were yours, Hark, but they were my own. I saved myself, Johnny. I saw myself dead in Amsterdam. I've come back from the dead. I'm clean.

PAUL: Amsterdam is not the capital of Holland.

DIDO: Everybody has a story, Sarah.

SARAH: That's the story, Dido.

PAUL: The Hague is the capital of Holland.

DIDO: Everybody has a story, Sarah.

PAUL: The European Court of Justice is in The Hague.

SARAH: Then tell them.

PAUL: There will be justice but there will be no peace without justice. Who said that? An Irishman said that. That's your only clue.

DIDO: You mean that's how I'll make money?

(SARAH *laughs*.)

You're right. Jesus, you're right. An everyday story of ordinary Derry ones. That's it. That's it.

PAUL: The Hague.

SARAH: I'm back, Johnny.

PAUL: Justice.

SARAH: I'm back.

PAUL: Peace with justice.

(SARAH *holds the dead bird.*)

SARAH: Poor bird. Bad wing. Never fly again. Bury it, Paul. In Derry. In the graveyard. In the pyramid. Wait for it to rise again. If what we saw is true, if the dead are to rise, then we must tell each other the truth. For us all to rise again.

(PAUL *takes the bird and places it in the pyramid.*)

SCENE FOUR

Thursday evening. MAELA *and* SEPH *are alone.*

MAELA: Do you sometimes hear things, Seph? I do, especially
when the other two go off for their walk. I hear things and
I think it's happening. There's never anything there of
course, but it doesn't stop me panicking. I panic very
easily. You're like me, aren't you? You're nervous.
(SEPH *shakes his head.*)
No? I thought you were. Are you afraid even?
(*Silence.*)
Of course you are. You should stop this silly nonsense, you
know. You should speak. Others did worse than you. Far
worse. And if you survived this long, then they'll let you
alone now.
(*Silence.*)
I wish the two of them were back. Can you imagine if it
happened and only you and me were here to see it? Who
would believe it? Ah, who cares? As long as it happened.
But I wouldn't want the others to miss it. You and Dido
and Paul as well. I think yous believe us. As for the other
boy, Harkin. What does a nice girl like Sarah see in that
brute?
(SEPH *shakes his head.*)
Oh, he's a brute all right, make no mistake. A bad, bad
boy. If my daughter walked into the house with that, he'd
be shown the door. Stay away from that kind of fella. Bad
news. Do you hear me? I want none of those kinds of boys
in my house. You'd think his stint suffering for his sins
would have cured him, but he's a bad boy, and he always
will be. Did you hear what Mr Harkin said to me
yesterday? He as good as called me a liar. Didn't he, Seph?
(*Silence.*)
I'm sorry, Seph. I can't control my mouth.

(SEPH *laughs*.)
Oh, laugh away. Go on. Or maybe I should laugh at you.
You couldn't control your mouth either. You don't like
that, do you? If you're going to laugh at other people, you
should learn to laugh at yourself. That's what I've learned.
I've also learned that life is very cruel. Isn't it, Seph?
(*Silence*.)
I wish them two bastards were back.
(*Silence*.)
I suppose you're shocked to hear me saying a word like
that, Seph.
(SEPH *shakes his head*.)
I am. I hate dirty words, though I love dirty stories. But I
hate dirty words. Dido has a way with words. He's very
smart.
(HARK *wheels on a barrow*. PAUL *enters with him*.)
I wonder what the surprise will be.

HARK: Surprise?

MAELA: You weren't here this morning. Dido said he would
have a surprise for us this evening.

HARK: What?

MAELA: He's definitely writing something.

HARK: Jesus.

MAELA: He's very smart, you know. Great in the quizzes, do
you remember, Paul?
(*Silence*.)
Paul knew everything.
(GRETA *and* SARAH *enter*.)

GRETA: You are not going to believe what is about to descend.
(DIDO *enters, in drag. He wears a long, flowing skirt, a loose
blouse, thick-rimmed glasses, boots and a beret. The pram is
crammed with objects*.)

DIDO: Hi.

MAELA: Sacred heart of the crucified Jesus.

DIDO: Do you like the new me?

MAELA: You walked through Derry looking like that?

DIDO: Yea, I got three wolf-whistles too. All from women.

Really, this town has gone to the dogs.

GRETA: Why are you dressed as a woman?

(*From the pram* DIDO *takes a neat pile of manuscripts. He hands one to* GRETA.)

DIDO: That's why.

GRETA: What's this?

DIDO: Read it.

GRETA: *The Burning Balaclava* by Fionnuala McGonigle. Who's Fionnuala McGonigle?

DIDO: You're looking at her, sweetheart. And it's pronounced (*fake French accent*) Fionn–u–ala Mc Gon–igle. She's French.

MAELA: With a name like Fionnuala McGonigle?

DIDO: *Oui*. I have come to your city and seen your suffering. Your city had just changed its name from Londonderry to Derry, and so I changed my name to Fionnuala in sympathy. What I see moves me so much I have written a small piece as my part of your struggle.

MAELA: Can we read it, Dido?

DIDO: Read it? You're going to do it. Hark, you play the heroine. She is a fifty-year-old Derry mother, tormented by the troubles, worn away by worry to a frizzle.

HARK: Why am I playing her?

DIDO: You have the looks for it. She is called Doherty.

HARK: Surprise, surprise. Everybody in Derry's called Doherty. It's a known fact.

GRETA: Nobody here's called Doherty.

HARK: It's still a well-known fact.

(DIDO *hands* HARK *an apron*.)

DIDO: Mrs Doherty has survived the troubles only through her fanatic devotion to the Sacred Heart.

(DIDO *hands* HARK *a statue of the Sacred Heart*.)

Sadly this devotion has led to the neglect of her son Padraig O Dochartaigh. He is a patriot and idealist. That's you, Maela, here.

(DIDO *hands* MAELA *a tricolour. It is gigantic*.)

Wrap it round you. Padraig is tormented by the troubles of

34

his native land. Should he or should he not take up the gun for Ireland? Should he or should he not speak Gaelic all the time? Should he or should he not screw his girlfriend, a Protestant, Mercy Dogherty. Paul, that's you. Here.

(DIDO *hands* PAUL *a long, blond wig.*)

PAUL: How am I a Protestant if I'm called Docherty?

DIDO: You spell Dogherty with a 'g'. You are a beautiful woman —

PAUL: I am a beautiful woman.

DIDO: A Protestant. A social worker. A good Protestant. You are tormented by your desire for a Catholic who might be involved, but you are reassured only by the fact that in bed he is all Protestant.

PAUL: How do you mean?

DIDO: Some people are Catholic in bed, some people are Protestant, some people convert, depending.

PAUL: Which is Catholic and which is Protestant?

DIDO: What a sheltered life you've led, dear. Mercy Dogherty is also tormented by guilt, because her father is an RUC man. That's you, Greta. Here.

(DIDO *hands* GRETA *rosary beads and a crucifix.*)

GRETA: What would an RUC man want with these?

DIDO: When he interrogates Catholic suspects he beats them over the head with the crucifix and strangles them with the rosary beads to make them confess. He's a brute. Now, Seph, I haven't forgotten you. You play a priest, Father O'Doherty. You are tormented because your weekly calls from the pulpit for peace and reconciliation have for so long gone unheard you have stopped speaking entirely and now communicate only by means of white flags. Here.

(DIDO *hands* SEPH *two large white sheets.*)

Wave them.

(SEPH *waves the white shirts together.*)

Perfect. Sarah, you play Jimmy Doherty, tormented —

HARK: There's a lot of torment in this.

DIDO: It's a tragedy, Hark, shut up. Jimmy is tormented by the fact that all his life he has been out of work. He's spent his time walking the dog and washing the wains and drinking in pubs telling yarns and singing songs. He's a Derry character but don't worry, he's the first to be killed. Here, Sarah.

(DIDO *hands* SARAH *a flat cap and a tattered raincoat.*)

I play two small parts myself. One is Doreen O'Doherty –

HARK: Tormented by –

DIDO: Driven to distraction by the troubles but as she is one of life's martyrs who never complains she is very kind to animals and goes nowhere without her pet dog, Charlie, on a lead. (*Produces a large, stuffed dog on a lead.*) I also play a British soldier, nameless, faceless, in enemy uniform, in deep torment because he is a working-class cockney sent here to oppress the working class. (*Brandishes a toy rifle.*) Now where are the other guns? The best I could rise to were water pistols, but we'll all need them for there's a shoot-out at the end. You'll need balaclavas as well. Watch the balaclavas. I had to borrow them from this Provo I know.

HARK: Why has he so many?

DIDO: He has a whole collection. It went to his head a bit when he came third in the terrorist of the year competition. You pose once in bathing costume, once in balaclava. It's supposed to be judged on military skills and revolutionary fervour, but the ones that win it tend to be a bunch of poseurs.

HARK: I never heard of a terrorist of the year.

DIDO: Jesus, Hark, you'll believe anything. Come on, get started. I'll read the directions as well as the two parts. Watch the scripts. Photocopies cost money.

MAELA: How did you afford them all, Dido?

DIDO: I gave a blow-job to a librarian in his lunch hour. He did them for me.

SARAH: You hang about libraries a lot, Dido.

DIDO: All human life is there, kid. Go. *The Burning Balaclava* by Fionnuala McGonigle. Our scene begins in a Derry kitchen. A Derry mother, that's you, Hark.

HARK: I know.

DIDO: Put on your apron. A Derry mother prays to the Sacred Heart.

HARK: Yes, Sacred Heart, how's it going? Sacred Heart, I envy you your life. There you are, stuck in a kitchen, and here's me worn down by the troubles of my native land. I don't know what I would do if I hadn't you for a bit of sport, Sacred Heart. You and me have some laughs together. But tell me anyway, what am I to do with my son? There's you with your fervent heart all burning with love for men, and here's me with my heart scalded, my heart is scalded by that young fella. I may as well talk to the wall as to him. Listen to this, Sacred Heart.

DIDO: Padraig O Dochartaigh enters. He is sullen and rough spoken.

MAELA: Is there any tea in the pot?

HARK: Forget about your belly for once. I'm making you no tea. Say a wee prayer with me to the Sacred Heart.

MAELA: Stuff your tea then, mother. I don't want your tea. We won't win our friends drinking tea. I refuse your tea.

HARK: I haven't offered you any.

MAELA: Don't contradict me, mother. Don't contradict a man driven to despair by what he sees. I see dead men and dead women. I see riots and confusion. I see my city in ruins.

HARK: God love you, did you see all that on TV?

MAELA: I see it with my own eyes, mother, my own eyes.

HARK: Turn your eyes to the Sacred Heart, son. He sees all.

DIDO: They look at the Sacred Heart. Padraig suddenly averts his eyes.

MAELA: Mother, not yet. I'm not ready to look at him yet.

HARK: All right, son. I'll make you a cup of tea.

DIDO: Our scene shifts to a Derry street. Doreen O'Doherty is walking with her dog Charlie. She meets Father O'Doherty. Hello, father.

(SEPH *waves a sheet.*)

'Isn't it a lovely day, father?'

(SEPH *waves a sheet.*)

I'll see you at Mass on Sunday, father. You preach a lovely sermon.

(SEPH *waves both sheets.*)

Bye-bye, father. Say a wee prayer for us all. Doreen sees a British soldier approaching. (*Pulls from the bag an army helmet.*) Oh Jesus, I'm supposed to be playing him as well. What'll I do? I'll just have to play both parts. There's nothing else for it. Right, here comes the Brit.

(*Playing the soldier,* DIDO *wears the helmet. Playing Doreen, he wears the beret.*)

'Where the fuck do you think you're going?' 'I'm going to the fish and chip shop with Charlie here. He's my wee hound of Ulster and he looks after me. I'm buying him a fish supper.' 'So you call your hound of Ulster fucking Charlie then? Here Charlie, Charlie, here fucking Charlie, Charlie.' (*Hops along with the stuffed dog.*) 'Look at the way he runs to you. Isn't it great the way animals know their own name? Give a paw, Charlie, give a paw.' 'I don't want his fucking paw.' 'Wait till you hear him singing. Sing a song Charlie, sing a wee song.' 'I don't want to hear any singing. I'm too deep in worry.' 'What are you worried about son?' 'Oh, the agony of being a working-class boy sent here to oppress the working class. Why did I do it? Why do I do it?' 'The money?' 'It's not worth it. It's not worth the money. I'm going to end it. I'm going to shoot myself.' 'Shoot me. Shoot me. Don't commit suicide.' 'I can't shoot you, madam. I'm a British soldier. We never shoot on sight. Tell you what. Is Charlie working class?' 'No, he's a cocker spaniel.' (*Shoots Charlie.*) 'Jesus Christ, you've shot Charlie. You've shot poor Charlie.' 'Maybe I can bring him back to life.' (*Starts to kick Charlie violently.*) 'What are you doing? What are you doing? You've killed him, now you're kicking the lining out of him.' 'Typical. Fucking typical of you Irish. We Brits never get any thanks.' 'I'm joining the IRA. I'm joining the IRA for Charlie.'

HARK: Doreen O'Doherty, did I hear you say you were joining

the IRA? Don't do it. I saw what they did to Charlie. But offer it up, Doreen. Offer it up to the Holy Souls in Purgatory. I know how it must break your heart. You've had Charlie since he was a young pup.

DIDO: I brought him home in a wee box, tied with string. I had to open it with a razor blade and I cut my finger. Little did I think that the pain I had bringing him into the house would be anything like the pain I have carrying him out of it.

HARK: Come on back and I'll make you a cup of tea.

DIDO: Thanks. I'll just have a cup in my hand.

HARK: A nice cup of tea.

DIDO: Our scene shifts to a Derry bar. Padraig and Mercy are drinking.

PAUL: Padraig?

MAELA: What, Mercy?

PAUL: Padraig, I am a beautiful woman.

MAELA: Mercy, you are some woman.

PAUL: But I am a demanding woman as well.

MAELA: You know your own mind, Mercy. You are a feminist.

PAUL: Do you know my mind, Padraig? For me, Padraig, would you burn your balaclava?

MAELA: What makes you think I wear a balaclava?

PAUL: I know, Padraig. I watch the news on TV. Oh, Padraig, what's going to happen to us? Where is there for people like us, a Protestant and a Catholic in love?

MAELA: There's a place for people like us.

PAUL: Somewhere.

MAELA: Sometime.

PAUL: Some place.

MAELA: A different place.

PAUL: A new place.

MAELA: A new province.

PAUL: A new province?

MAELA: A province where Catholics and Protestants can go to bed together and talk dirty.

PAUL: I think I'm going to cry.

MAELA: Mercy, remember, feminists don't cry.

DIDO: Mercy and Padraig look at each other. It is love.

PAUL: It's your round, Padraig.

MAELA: I got the last one.

PAUL: No, you didn't.

MAELA: I did. We've had three, I got the first.

PAUL: Padraig, why do we always end up fighting? Do you hate me because I'm Protestant?

MAELA: Of course not. I'm a Catholic, how could I be a bigot? But your father is an RUC man. You know what you must do.

PAUL: No, no, oh no, no.

MAELA: Yes, yes, oh yes, yes.

DIDO: Our scene shifts to an RUC interrogation centre.

GRETA: Who exactly are you, mister?

SARAH: Sure everybody knows me, Jimmy Doherty.

GRETA: What's your religion, Jimmy?

SARAH: Religion, religion, isn't it a great thing, religion? Where would we be buried if it weren't for religion?

GRETA: Together.

SARAH: Aye, in death, as in life, apart. Why have you hauled me in here?

GRETA: To beat you up.

SARAH: Sure I never refuse a body. Away you go.

(GRETA *beats* SARAH's *head with a crucifix*.)

GRETA: What's your politics?

SARAH: The man in the street's.

(GRETA *throttles* SARAH *with the rosary beads*.)

GRETA: I want this man's name and address. What do you do? Who do you work for?

SARAH: I sing songs and tell wee jokes. Have you never heard me? (*Sings:*) 'In my memory I will always be – '

(GRETA *pulls her water pistol*.)

GRETA: One more note and you're dead.

SARAH: 'In the town that I love so well.'

(GRETA *shoots* SARAH.)

You'll never get away with this.

GRETA: I was putting you out of your misery. No jury of sane men or women would convict me.

(SARAH *dies dramatically*.)

DIDO: Just die, Sarah.

GRETA: Do I kill anybody else?

MAELA: Dido, isn't there enough killing on the streets of Derry without bringing it into the graveyard?

DIDO: On with the play. Our scene shifts to the Waterside. A Catholic priest walks through Protestant areas on his mission of peace.

(SEPH *walks across, waving white sheets*.)

In their Protestant home Mercy has told Daddy she is to marry a Catholic. She is weeping.

PAUL: So you see, Daddy, I have a terrible choice.

GRETA: About your future family's religion?

PAUL: Yes, Daddy. The Catholic church will never agree to me bringing them up as children.

GRETA: Don't you mean Protestant?

PAUL: No, Daddy. Catholics are conceived at the age of forty. That way there's no sex. What am I going to do, Daddy? I love him.

GRETA: Kill him.

DIDO: Our scene shifts. Quick, everybody, pistols and balaclavas. Not you, Hark. You're in the middle of an ambush. Run through it with the Sacred Heart. Squirt, everybody, squirt. Run, Hark. Get the Sacred Heart. Get the Sacred Heart. Drop him, Hark. Drop him.

(HARK *drops the statue of the Sacred Heart and it breaks*.)

Stop the fight. Our scene changes to a Derry kitchen. Mrs Doherty nurses her broken Sacred Heart. Padraig enters.

MAELA: Ma, ma, has there been an ambush?

HARK: There's been an ambush, son. Look, look.

MAELA: Ma, your Sacred Heart.

HARK: My Sacred Heart, son, my Sacred Heart. Son, son, where were you when my Sacred Heart was riddled with bullets? Where were you?

MAELA: I was having a quick pint with the girlfriend, ma.

HARK: Take away these quick pints, take away these girl–
  Girlfriend? Who?

MAELA: I meant to tell you about Mercy –

HARK: Mercy? She's a Protestant with a name like that.

MAELA: I want to marry her, ma. I love her. What will I do?

HARK: Kill her.

MAELA: That's dirty, ma.

HARK: It's your duty as a Catholic.

MAELA: Ah ma, no.

HARK: Then do it for me, son. Do it for your mother.

MAELA: All right.

DIDO: Our scene changes. A Derry street. On one side Mrs
  Doherty and Padraig, on the other Mercy and her
  Protestant Daddy.
  (DIDO *produces a cassette recorder and plays 'Do not forsake
  me, O my darling' from* High Noon. *They both wave water
  pistols.*)
  As they move in, a priest appears, along with a British
  soldier.
  (SEPH *wanders between both parties, waving white sheets.*)
  They fire. They get the priest.
  (*The white sheets fall.* SEPH *dies.*)

MAELA: We've shot a priest, we've shot a priest.

PAUL: He's not a priest, he's not a priest.

MAELA: How is he not a priest?

PAUL: He's not waving a white flag.
  (MAELA *shoots* PAUL.)

MAELA: Blasphemer, you've shot a priest.
  (GRETA *shoots* MAELA.)

GRETA: Catholic bastard, you've shot my daughter.
  (HARK *shoots* GRETA.)

HARK: You murdering RUC madman. Look at this. All dead.
  Dead. What could I do? I had to kill. I depend on the
  dying. Nobody knew it, not even my son, but I knit all the
  balaclavas. The more that dies, the more I'm given.
  Violence is terrible, but it pays well.
  (DIDO *shoots* HARK.)

42

DIDO: What could I do? I'm only a soldier. A working-class boy, just a boy. What does Ireland mean to me? What does it all mean?

(*They all rise and shoot* DIDO.)

They've got me. I join the dying. What's a Brit under the clay? What's a Protestant in the ground? What's a Catholic in the grave? All the same. Dead. All dead. We're all dead. I'm dying. They've got me. It's over. It's over. (*Dies.*)

That's it. What did you think?

(*Silence.*)

Tell me the truth. Isn't it just like real life?

(*Silence.*)

Did yous like it?

HARK: I'm searching for words to describe it.

DIDO: Did you think it was too short?

HARK: It's not short. It's shite.

(HARK *hurls the script and the apron at* DIDO.)

Shite.

SARAH: Dido, you know Hark. He can be a rough man. He just says things straight out. I think this time he's right. It's shite.

(SARAH *throws her script and props at* DIDO.)

PAUL: Shite incredible.

GRETA: Shite incarnate.

(*They throw their scripts and props at* DIDO. SEPH *throws his script and sheets at* DIDO *also.*)

MAELA: Dido, there's some people who take great delight in running other people down. You have great courage, I think. If I'd written that shite, I wouldn't show my face for a month.

(MAELA *hurls in her script and flag.*)

HARK: Your skirt's lovely though. It suits you.

DIDO: Borrow it, shitehawk, borrow it.

(DIDO *tears off the skirt and throws it at* HARK.)

Fuck yous.

(DIDO *crams the stuffed dog and the overcoat and cap into the pram.*)

43

Fuck yous.

(DIDO *puts the apron and wig into the pram and exits.*)

SARAH: Can I borrow your beret?

(DIDO *throws the beret to* SARAH.)

GRETA: The blouse might suit me.

(DIDO *hurls the blouse to* GRETA.)

DIDO: Fuck yous.

(DIDO *stuffs more objects into the pram, leaving behind the water pistols, religious images and balaclavas.*)

Fuck yous. Fuck yous.

(DIDO *exits.*)

HARK: Well, that was crack.

MAELA: It wasn't that bad, was it?

HARK: Even old Seph enjoyed himself. Good old Seph. A great laugh.

SEPH: Can I have a cigarette?

(*Silence.*)

Can I have a cigarette?

HARK: Nobody smokes.

SEPH: Can I have a cigarette?

(GRETA *takes out a cigarette and hands it to* SEPH. HARK *grabs the cigarette and breaks it into pieces, speaking:*)

HARK: Long, short, long, short, long, short. Pick a straw, Seph. Pick one. Long or short. Live or die. Eat or starve. Do you remember, Seph? Has your tongue gone on strike? Are you not speaking? Are you not smoking? Are you not eating? (*Empties the cigarette from his hands.*) You'll kill yourself, Seph. Smoking.

(*Silence.*)

SEPH: Can I have a cigarette?

PAUL: Give him a cigarette.

(GRETA *hands* SEPH *another cigarette.*)

Why have you come home, Seph?

(*Silence.*)

SARAH: Tell us.

SEPH: I talked. I ran away. And I came back. I went to those I informed on. I said, 'Kill me. Let me die.' They said,

'Live. That's your sentence. Life, not death. Live with
what you've done.'

PAUL: Why did you come back here to die?

SARAH: Why did you come back here to live?

SEPH: I lived here, I was born here. I was here one Sunday.
Sunday. I saw it. Bloody Sunday. I was in Derry on Bloody
Sunday.

GRETA: Bloody Sunday. Where were you on Bloody Sunday?

PAUL: Here. I was here.

HARK: On the march.

SARAH: Through Derry.

GRETA: Were we all there?

(*Silence.*)

Were we all here on Bloody Sunday?

SEPH: Everything changed after Bloody Sunday.

MAELA: Nothing changed. Nothing happened that day. Nobody
died. I should know. I was in the hospital. If there had
been anyone dead I would have seen them, and I saw no
one dead. You're telling lies. You've driven away the dead.
I hope you're satisfied. I hope you're satisfied with your
lies.

(MAELA *rushes out.*)

SARAH: Where's she going?

GRETA: Maela, Maela.

SARAH: Follow her.

(DIDO *appears.*)

DIDO: Leave her.

(*Silence.*)

Leave her alone.

(*Silence.*)

Leave her.

(*Silence.*)

SCENE FIVE

Friday morning. GRETA *and* SARAH *are alone.* GRETA *fingers Maela's knitting.*

SARAH: Do you like Hark, Greta?

GRETA: I don't know him.

SARAH: Who does?

GRETA: Paul.

SARAH: Old mates.

GRETA: Old pals.

SARAH: Yea. Friends. Them and Seph, they knocked about
together. Reunited. Funny life, eh?

GRETA: Hysterical.
(*Silence.*)
Have you come back for him?

SARAH: Yes.

GRETA: Do you think he'll save you?

SARAH: What from?

GRETA: Yourself.

SARAH: He has to save himself first.

GRETA: Does he?

SARAH: We all have.

GRETA: Are we worth saving?
(*Silence.*)
Do we ever get what we want?

SARAH: What makes you ask that?

GRETA: When I was a girl, the one thing I wanted most was a
brother.

SARAH: You have no brother?

GRETA: What makes you think I had?

SARAH: The song you keep singing.

GRETA: (*Laughs.*) The song? No, I've no brother. I thought I
had once. A brother.

SARAH: How?

GRETA: I just imagined it.

SARAH: Who was he?

GRETA: Myself.

(GRETA *laughs*.)

SARAH: Share the joke.

GRETA: Do you remember the first time the moon touched you? Did you know what was happening?

SARAH: Just about.

GRETA: Jesus, I didn't. I didn't know what was happening. And you know what I did? I asked my father. Can you believe that? The poor man nearly died. He murmured about my mother. My mother was cracked, Sarah. Cracked. Talk about houseproud, she wallpapered the dustbin. Our house was so clean people called it the doll's house. They used to come and look in our windows. The woman polished the footpath. Cracked. Anyway, I asked my mother. When ma wanted to tell you anything secret, she would go under the table and whisper it to you there. She did that up to her dying day and she spent more and more time under the table because she began to find things more and more secret. Anyway, I digress. There we were under the table and my mother told me I was bleeding because of the fairies.

SARAH: The fairies?

GRETA: The fairies. There are good fairies and bad fairies and the good fairies come to good little girls and give them two gifts. (*Points to her breasts*.) But the bad fairies give little girls blood. She had a bandage and I would be right as rain in no time. I was fourteen, I knew nothing, but I did know my mother was out of her tree. So what was happening? I thought about it, and then it hit me. I thought I was turning into a man. My bleeding was a sure sign. I was certain the next thing after the breasts and the blood would be I'd grow a beard. For months afterwards, whenever I was lonely, I'd touch my breasts, and say, at least I'll soon have a brother and he'll be myself. I grew out of that, I hope.

47

SARAH: Are they dead, your parents?

GRETA: Yea. I still live in their house on my own. It's not a doll's house any more. Anybody who looks in my window wishes they hadn't. Sorry, mother. I'm not the most pleasant of women.

SARAH: Good.

GRETA: Good.

(*They laugh.* SARAH *reaches for* GRETA's *hand and kisses it.*) What's that for?

SARAH: A gift from the good fairy.

GRETA: Fuck the good fairy.

SARAH: She's better than nothing.

GRETA: She certainly is.

SARAH: Was it one of them appeared to you, your father or mother?

GRETA: I appeared to myself.

(*Silence.*)

Christ, I hope they find Maela.

SARAH: Dido will find her.

GRETA: When he's in his right mind, Paul's more reliable. He might handle her better.

SARAH: We'll find her. Hark and Seph are searching the graveyard. Do you think she's stopped believing?

(*Silence.*)

Have you stopped believing?

GRETA: No, Sarah, no.

(DIDO *and* PAUL *enter.* MAELA *is linked to both.*)

Maela, thank Christ.

DIDO: Let her be.

MAELA: Let me go.

DIDO: Maela, I'm going off to get you some warm tea. Do you want that?

MAELA: I want nothing. She's dead, isn't she?

(*Silence.*)

My wee girl's dead. They're running mad through the streets of Derry and my daughter's dead. Do you not understand that?

CARTHAGINIANS

DIDO: Understand what, Maela?

(SEPH *and* HARK *enter.* MAELA *starts to walk about the burial stones, touching them as she speaks.*)

Where are you going, Maela?

MAELA: Nowhere. Nowhere. I went for a walk. Through Derry. Everybody was crying. What was wrong with them? All shouting. I couldn't hear what. Was it at me? I wasn't listening to them.

DIDO: What were you listening to?

MAELA: They said, 'She's dead. I'm afraid she's dead. We can get you home safely in an ambulance. There's a lot of bother stirring in the town.' I said, 'What do you mean she's dead? There is a dead thing in there and that thing is cancer, that thing is not my daughter. My daughter's at home. I better get back to her. I don't know what I'm doing out. The town's gone mad today, hasn't it?

DIDO: She's dead, Maela, your daughter's dead.

MAELA: No, doctor, you're wrong. My daughter is alive. My daughter is not that thing. I'm going home.

DIDO: I'll go with you.

MAELA: Nonsense. I'm perfectly capable of walking home. At my age I should know my way round Derry. I've walked through it often enough. William Street and Shipquay Street and Ferryquay Street and the Strand and Rosville Street and Great James Street. I'm walking home through my own city. Everybody's running and everybody's crying. What's wrong? Why cry? Two dead, I hear that in William Street. I'm walking through Derry and they're saying in Shipquay Street there's five dead. I am walking to my home in my house in the street I was born in and I've forgotten where I live. I am in Ferryquay Street and I hear there's nine dead outside the Rosville flats. They opened fire and shot them dead. No, nobody's dead. My daughter's not dead. I'm not dead. Where are there dead in Derry? Let me look on the dead. Jesus, the dead. The innocent dead. There's thirteen dead in Derry. (*Stumbles from stone to stone.*) Where do I stand? Where am I? What

49

day is it? Sunday. Why is the sun bleeding? It's pouring blood. I want a priest. Get me a priest. Where am I? In Great James Street. It's full of chemists. I need a tonic for my nerves. For my head. For my heart. Pain in my heart. Breaking heart. I've lost one. I've lost them all. They had no hair. She had fire. She opened fire on herself. When I wasn't looking she caught cancer. It burned her. She was thirteen. It was Sunday. I have to go to Mass. I have to go to Mass. I have to go to Mass, Dido, take me to Mass, Dido. Take me out, Dido. Take me out of myself.

DIDO: Who wrote *The Firebird*, Maela?

(*Silence.*)

Who, Maela?

MAELA: No.

PAUL: *The Firebird*, who wrote it, Maela?

MAELA: Stravinsky.

PAUL: What nationality?

MAELA: Russian.

DIDO: Where is the *Venus de Milo*?

MAELA: Paris. She has no arms.

DIDO: Someday we'll head for Paris, Maela. We'll learn French.

(MAELA *nods.* DIDO *strokes her hand.*)

Where do we live, Maela?

MAELA: That's a hard one.

DIDO: Do you want a clue? Derry is —

MAELA: Doire. Doire Colmcille.

DIDO: What does that mean?

MAELA: The dove. The bird of peace.

DIDO: Where do we live in Derry?

MAELA: The graveyard.

DIDO: Why?

MAELA: It seems to be where we belong.

DIDO: Every question correct, Maela.

PAUL: You're some woman.

DIDO: No stopping her.

MAELA: Is it over?

DIDO: Not to the final.

MAELA: Will we make it?

DIDO: What do you say, Paul?

PAUL: Oldie and Goldie are back in action.

DIDO: Get the questions ready, Paul.

HARK: I'm game.

DIDO: Thanks, Hark. The rest of you?
> (*They nod.*)
> Maela, you're not to get drunk before it starts. Bottle of
> sherry, dry?
> (MAELA *nods.*)
> The rest of yous?

HARK: Couple of six-packs?

SEPH: Aye.

GRETA: Vodka?

SARAH: Tonic?

PAUL: Nothing for me.

DIDO: Couple of Britvic 55s?

PAUL: OK.

DIDO: Throw in what's going. Remember the small
commission.

MAELA: You have a heart like a cash register, young fella.

DIDO: Ring-a-ding, dear, ring-a-ding. Give us your money.
> (*Money is thrown at* DIDO.)

SCENE SIX

Friday evening. In darkness the sound of football rattles. Light rises to find them in party mood. Wearing white and red scarves, MAELA, DIDO *and* HARK *wave football rattles.*

HARK: Give me a D.
CHORUS: D.
HARK: Give me an E.
CHORUS: E.
HARK: Give me an R.
CHORUS: R.
HARK: Give me another one.
CHORUS: R.
HARK: Give me a Y.
CHORUS: Y.
HARK: What have you got?
CHORUS: Rubbish.
      (*The football rattles go frantic.*)
PAUL: Order, order, order.
HARK: (*Sings.*) The referee's a bastard, a bastard, a bastard,
      The referee's a bastard, e–i–o.
      (PAUL *shows* HARK *the yellow card.*)
      What did I do? What did I do?
      (HARK *appeals innocently to the others.*)
CHORUS: The referee's a bastard, a bastard, a bastard.
      The referee's a bastard, e–i–o.
PAUL: OK, I give up, I give up.
CHORUS: Booooo.
PAUL: Roar among yourselves for a while. I'm sorting out
      questions.
HARK: Paul, where was the last time we were in a shower like
      this?
PAUL: The one and only pub.
HARK: Not the Derry Renaissance?

PAUL: Where else, big fella?

DIDO: What Derry Renaissance?

HARK: The Derry Renaissance was strictly confined to pubs. Correction, one pub.

DIDO: Which pub?

HARK: You wouldn't remember it. It was closed down.

DIDO: Was it raided?

PAUL: Yea.

DIDO: By the army?

HARK: No.

DIDO: Police?

PAUL: No.

DIDO: Who raided it then?

SEPH: Cruelty-to-animals people.

DIDO: What?

SEPH: It was closed over a cat.

PAUL: Mustard Arse.

HARK: Poor Mustard Arse.

DIDO: Who was Mustard Arse?

SEPH: The cat that closed the pub.

DIDO: How could a cat close a pub?

PAUL: That's a story in itself.

DIDO: Tell us.

PAUL: It was a rough place.

SEPH: Rough owner.

HARK: Not that rough, he loved the cat.

SEPH: Siamese, beautiful.

HARK: Grey, great colour, moved like a dancer, in and out the glasses on the counter, graceful. That was its downfall.

DIDO: Its grace?

HARK: Not exactly. Some rough customers drunk there. How did we survive holding arts evenings?

SEPH: We were together.

PAUL: They served brilliant sandwiches.

HARK: Great chunks of ham, thick as your fist.

PAUL: One day this big guy eating a sandwich asked for the mustard.

SEPH: Cat came waltzing along the counter.

HARK: Your man sticks the knife into the mustard.

SEPH: Cat walks past, tail in the air.

PAUL: Your man spreads a streak of mustard on the cat's arse.

HARK: Cat went bananas.

SEPH: Leaps from the counter into an alcove.

HARK: A stag's head's hanging in the alcove.

PAUL: Hanging on to the wall by a nail.

SEPH: Cat starts rubbing its arse on the head.

HARK: The rubbing dislodges the nail.

SEPH: The head falls on these three old fellas.

HARK: They're sitting in their usual corner under the head.

PAUL: Kills one outright.

SEPH: Knocks the other two senseless.

HARK: The cat's still going bananas.

SEPH: Send an ambulance.

PAUL: Send a priest.

HARK: Send a fucking vet.

PAUL: All arrived at the one time.

SEPH: The vet got the place closed down.

HARK: We did our bit as well. Paul was compere, Seph played the guitar, and I was the poet – Jesus, can you imagine that?

(DIDO *has a bowl of lemon slices and salt before him. Ostentatiously he pours salt on to his hand, lifts a slice of lemon and slugs back his drink, followed by the lemon and salt.*)

GRETA: What the hell are you drinking?

DIDO: Tequila.

GRETA: What's it like?

DIDO: It's rotten, but it's great for the image.

GRETA: Are you going to drink that the whole evening?

DIDO: No way, I've got a six-pack of Guinness for when I want a drink.

GRETA: Are you OK for vodka over there, Sarah?

SARAH: Grand, thanks, Greta.

GRETA: Just come over here and help yourself –

DIDO: She will not come over here.

MAELA: She will not come over here.

DIDO: There's no conferring between teams.

MAELA: There's no conferring between teams.

GRETA: Are you two parrots?

MAELA: Come over here, have you ever heard the like?

DIDO: Amateurs. Why have we got her on the team?

MAELA: Think of her as a kind of mascot.

DIDO: Yea, a big cat. We'll call her Fluffy.

(MAELA *and* DIDO *roar laughing.*)

MAELA: God forgive us, Greta, we're just taking a hand at you.

GRETA: Are yous?

DIDO: Listen, Greta, you better know how we work. Maela answers on literature, mythology, art, music –

MAELA: I do classical, Dido does pop.

DIDO: I also do sport, current affairs, film, geography and history, Roman and Renaissance being my two strongest areas.

GRETA: What am I supposed to do?

DIDO: You just sit there and look fluffy.

(MAELA *and* DIDO *go hysterical.*)

GRETA: I'm warning you two bastards.

DIDO: No, seriously, we're weak in cookery and cricket.

SARAH: We haven't a hope in hell.

HARK: We are going to pulverize those two bigheads.

PAUL: Are we ready to kick off?

HARK: Fire away, Paul.

DIDO: Hark, if your team needs a few points' start –

HARK: How's your balls, queer boy?

DIDO: Swinging. How's yours?

HARK: Stiff.

DIDO: Jesus, listen to once in a lifetime.

PAUL: Team questions. Hark's team, what was the size of the crowd at last year's FA Cup Final?

HARK: A hundred thousand.

PAUL: Near enough. A hundred thousand attended the final. Name them, Dido's team?

55

DIDO: What?

PAUL: You have ten seconds; ten, nine, eight, seven, six, five –

HARK: – four, three, two, one, zero.

PAUL: I won't pass it over. Dido's team, in the 1963 film, *Cleopatra*, a well-known couple –

DIDO: I know this. Elizabeth –

PAUL: – Taylor and Richard Burton were the leads. Cleopatra died by means of an asp bite. What was the name of the asp?

GRETA: Would it be Doris?

DIDO: How the hell would it be Doris?

GRETA: Maybe it was Sammy?

PAUL: Sammy is correct. All equal. Einstein's Theory of Relativity –

DIDO: I need a bottle of Guinness.

PAUL: Einstein's Theory of Relativity has never been set to music. Four points for the first version.

HARK: (*Sings.*) I woke up this morning, I had something in my head.
I woke up this morning, was it something I had said?
What was that something? Would I find it in bed?
I looked out my window, I see e equals mc squared.
I looked out my window, I see e equals mc squared.
I tell you, baby. I got the Theory of Relativity blues.

PAUL: Beautiful, Hark, beautiful. Dido's team, who captained the 1971 Arsenal League and FA Cup double champions?

MAELA: Frank McClintock.

DIDO: Hold it, Maela, that's enough.

MAELA: It was Frank McClintock.

DIDO: That's enough, Maela. Paul, I demand to answer that question. It's not fair to expect poor Maela to answer a football question.

PAUL: How do the opposition feel about that?

HARK: Let him answer.

DIDO: Thank you, Hark. A nice touch from the opposition. 'Seventy-one, Arsenal Double team, let me think, captain, Charlie George?

PAUL: Wrong. Other team?

HARK: Frank McClintock.

PAUL: Correct.

DIDO: You dirty bollocks.

HARK: Thank you, Dido. Nice touch from the opposition.

DIDO: Shut up, Hark.

MAELA: I knew that, Dido.

DIDO: Shut up, Maela.

PAUL: Easy one. Which queen of Carthage ruled there until deserted by Aeneas?

DIDO: Dido, Queen of Carthage.

HARK: Dido, queen of Derry.

DIDO: At least I admit it, sunshine.

HARK: Bitch, bitch.

PAUL: Hark's team, what does Carthage mean?
   (*They confer.*)

HARK: We don't know.

DIDO: It means new city.

PAUL: Correct.

MAELA: You know a lot about Carthage, Dido.

DIDO: (*Whispers:*) I know a lot about the question master, Maela.
   (*They nudge each other.*)

PAUL: I declare the quiz a draw. Congratulations.
   (*The football rattles go.*)

DIDO: Tie-breaker, tie-breaker, we demand a tie-breaker.

PAUL: Hark's team, which admiral died at the Battle of Trafalgar?

HARK: Nelson.

PAUL: Dido's team, who else died at the same battle?
   (*Silence.*)

DIDO: Was there a Sammy?

PAUL: Wrong.
   (*Cheers from Hark's team.*)

SCENE SEVEN

Saturday afternoon. MAELA *knits.* GRETA *smokes.* PAUL *constructs the pyramid.* SEPH *nurses the guitar, occasionally running his fingers along the strings, tunelessly.* HARK *and* SARAH *sit together,* DIDO *resting between them, his head on* SARAH'S *lap, his hand around* HARK'S *leg.*

DIDO: I speak only for myself, but I found the experience wonderful. Intimate, sharing, sweet. It was so gentle and beautiful. We must do it again, just the three of us, together.

HARK: Do what?

DIDO: Share a Mars bar together. The most gorgeous Mars bar of all time.

HARK: Did you ever hear two's company?

DIDO: Yea, but three's practical.

GRETA: 'I had only one brother, God rest his soul.'

SARAH: I want a kid, Hark.

GRETA: 'He was drowned in the river . . .'

SARAH: I'd like a kid.

HARK: Here and now?

SARAH: I'd like a child.

HARK: Put it out of your head.

SARAH: Think about it.

HARK: It's not going to happen.

DIDO: What do you want a kid for? Haven't you got me? Adopt me.

HARK: I'll think about the kid, Sarah.

DIDO: On top of everything else, now I've to cope with parental rejection. Again.

MAELA: What did your own do to reject you?

DIDO: They run away.

GRETA: 'Only one brother, God rest . . . drowned in the river . . .'

58

(*Silence.*)

HARK: Maybe.

SARAH: Maybe.

HARK: We'll see.

GRETA: Are you telling the truth, Sarah?

SARAH: About the child?

GRETA: Is it the truth? Wasn't it your big idea to tell the truth?

PAUL: Leave her alone.

GRETA: Why?

PAUL: Just leave her.

GRETA: Why do you go mad, Paul?

HARK: Leave him, Greta.

GRETA: Leave him. Leave her. Leave me to tell the truth. What about telling the truth?

HARK: What do you want to know?

PAUL: I go mad when I have to.

GRETA: 'Have to'?

PAUL: Leave me alone.

GRETA: Stop building that stupid thing. What are you going to do with it?

PAUL: Be buried in it. With the dead. When they rise.

GRETA: You're talking like a madman.

MAELA: Long ago they talked of washing the dead. It was for the Last Judgement. For them rising.

GRETA: Can the dead rise?

PAUL: You saw them rising, not me.

GRETA: Was I mad when I saw it?

PAUL: Stop talking about madness.

(GRETA *starts to rip the black plastic bag apart.*)

Stop. Stop it.

(*She continues.*)

Stop.

GRETA: Why, Paul? What's in it?

PAUL: The dead. That's where I find them.

GRETA: Why are they in there?

PAUL: Hiding.

GRETA: From what?

PAUL: The war.

GRETA: What war?

PAUL: In my head. The war in my head. It's driven me mad.

HARK: There's another war outside your head.

PAUL: It's driving me mad. I'm losing a grip on myself.

HARK: A war I fought.

PAUL: I was a good teacher. I was popular with people.

HARK: And I fought it for good reason.

PAUL: I run two quizzes in different pubs to save a bit of money. I want to see Egypt. I want to go to Carthage. But I'm losing a grip on myself. I don't want to go mad.

SEPH: Why are you mad, Paul?

PAUL: Derry destroyed.

HARK: For good reason.

PAUL: Every bullet, every boot put through it –

HARK: For good reason.

PAUL: I've felt them all.

SEPH: Can you feel any more?

PAUL: The pain comes and goes and I go mad with pain. The living can't heal it, but the dead might. I believe they'll rise because I am mad, for if the dead don't rise to meet me –

HARK: Enough.

PAUL: I will meet them for I cannot last much longer in this town.

GRETA: Why the hell do you put yourself through this?
(*Silence.*)
I don't believe you're mad. I don't believe you. I think you're full of lies. Full of shit.

HARK: And you're not?

GRETA: If I am, I don't go around squealing for pity.

HARK: But you go around squealing for truth?

GRETA: Why shouldn't I?

SEPH: Be full of pity?

MAELA: Why would you want pity, Greta?

SEPH: For being herself. She hates herself.

GRETA: Do I, traitor?

SEPH: Being a traitor –

GRETA: And you are.

SEPH: I know. I know what I am. I hauled this from the mast and I danced on it. (*Grabs the discarded tricolour from* The Burning Balaclava.) That's the way I made sense of it all.

PAUL: Made sense?

SEPH: Would it have been better to have been shot on Bloody Sunday? Did I want that to happen? Why did I want that? Why did we all want it? Did we want Bloody Sunday to happen?

PAUL: How did we want Bloody Sunday?

SEPH: To make sense of it all, make sense, Paul. (*Starts to wrap the tricolour around the guitar.*) Thirteen dead on Bloody Sunday. It could have been thirteen hundred. Thirteen thousand. Thirteen million. One. One left alive, that one is me and I'm going to tell.

PAUL: You've told enough.

SEPH: Have I told this to you? Listen. (*Batters the ground with the guitar wrapped in the tricolour.*) That's the war in my head. They said after Bloody Sunday they wanted to avenge the dead but they wanted to join them. And I would tell on the living who wanted to join the dead. I'd save them from themselves. I'd save them from the dead. I would tell before I died –

HARK: You were a traitor. Nothing else. Who gives a damn if you live or die?

PAUL: Do you give a damn who lives or dies now?

HARK: No.

SARAH: You did one time.

HARK: Long ago.

DIDO: What changed you?

HARK: I changed myself. That's life, eh, Sarah?

PAUL: No, that's luck.

HARK: Pick a straw, the luck of the straw. The loser goes hungry, the loser goes on strike.

PAUL: You never went hungry.

HARK: Pick the long straw, pick the short straw.

PAUL: You were never on the strike.

HARK: I got the long straw.

PAUL: You never volunteered.

HARK: I didn't go hungry.

PAUL: You didn't want to.

HARK: I didn't die.

PAUL: Lucky boy, eh?

DIDO: Do you not eat at all, Hark?

HARK: Very refined stomach.

PAUL: You lived, Harkin. Others died. You never volunteered.

HARK: Things tend to go down the wrong way.

PAUL: What did Seph know to tell but what we all know?

HARK: I find myself vomiting a lot.

PAUL: What were you, Harkin?

(HARK *grabs some of the water pistols*.)

A glorified look-out man who got himself caught.

(HARK *starts to shoot with the water pistols*.)

What have you done we haven't all done?

HARK: Coward.

(HARK *continues to shoot*.)

PAUL: Big hero, Harkin. Hard man.

HARK: Coward.

PAUL: Somebody's coming, Johnny.

HARK: Hide.

PAUL: Eat, Johnny. Enjoy yourself.

HARK: Hide.

PAUL: You never used the gun, Hark. Give it to me.

HARK: I want to use it, Paul.

PAUL: Give it to me. It's only a toy.

HARK: Not a toy. A gun.

PAUL: Give me the gun. Free yourself.

HARK: Free Ireland.

(PAUL *grabs* HARK's *hand with the gun and raises the hand to* HARK's *mouth*.)

PAUL: Eat it then. Eat before I shove it down you throat.

(HARK *throws* PAUL's *hand away*.)

HARK: Can't. Coward. Can't fire. Can't kill. Can't eat.

(HARK *breaks the gun. He lifts both parts to his mouth and bites on them. He spits them out.*)
Must kill. Can't kill. Can't eat. Must eat. Want to live. Jesus, go away and die, leave me alone. All I could have killed was myself. I couldn't. Now, Sarah, bad as you. Leave me alone. Come back. Come back to me. I'm dead. Come back and raise the dead.

SARAH: All right.

HARK: Told the truth.

GRETA: Tell a joke.

HARK: Tell the truth, Greta. You said it.

GRETA: Tell a dirty joke.

HARK: Tell the truth.

GRETA: A doctor joke. A woman walks into a doctor's office. A woman walks into a doctor's office.

SARAH: She says, 'Doctor, doctor — '

GRETA: 'I've a pain.' He says, 'Speak up.'

MAELA: She says, 'I've a pain.'

GRETA: He says, 'Speak up, speak up.'

MAELA: A pain.

GRETA: Where?

MAELA: So she points.

(GRETA *does not move.*)

SARAH: When do you get the pain?

GRETA: Just before the moon touches.

MAELA: And she knows there's something wrong?

GRETA: She always knew something would go wrong, every time before she bled. They put her into hospital and there she starts to laugh.

SARAH: Why?

GRETA: She deserved what was done to her.

MAELA: Why?

GRETA: She didn't know why the moon touched her and she'll never bleed again. She called her blood her brother. She's lost her blood and her brother. She saw the dead, she saw nothing for she saw herself and she is nothing. She's not a woman any more. She's a joke. A dirty joke. She has no pity any more. (*Gathers the remains of the plastic sack about herself.*)

'I had only one brother, may God rest his soul.

He was drowned in the river. In the river.'

SARAH: Greta.

(*Silence.*)

Greta.

(SARAH *goes to* GRETA. *She opens* GRETA's *shirt and puts her hands on* GRETA's *breasts.*)

GRETA: It's a sin.

SARAH: No sin.

GRETA: It's tonight, Sarah.

SARAH: I know.

MAELA: So do I.

GRETA: They will rise tonight, the dead will rise tonight.

SCENE EIGHT

Saturday night. They sit in a circle.

DIDO: Do you ever get afraid in this place?
GRETA: What of?
DIDO: Ghosts and things?
GRETA: Do you believe in ghosts?
DIDO: Yes. Do you?
GRETA: Why do you think we're here?
    (*Silence.*)
DIDO: I'm scared shitless.
    (*Silence.*)
    I hope they're not going to be poltergeists. I saw a film
    about a poltergeist. It bit people's heads off and
    disembowelled them. I had to be nearly carried out of the
    cinema every time I saw it.
SARAH: How often did you see it?
DIDO: Five times. It was brilliant.
HARK: You have great taste in films.
DIDO: Yea, I know. I see everything.
HARK: Nothing like a good western.
DIDO: When you were a kid, Hark, playing Cowboys and
    Indians, which were you?
HARK: The Indian.
DIDO: You get weirder by the minute.
HARK: What's wrong with Indians?
DIDO: They always got beaten.
HARK: Not always.
SEPH: I liked the Indians as well. Their head-dresses were
    great.
HARK: They had the best words.
PAUL: Firewater.
HARK: Medicine man.
SEPH: Peace pipe.

PAUL: Great words. Like poetry.

SEPH: Do you ever write poetry, Hark?

HARK: I wrote doggerel.

PAUL: Some good stuff. Heady days back then.

GRETA: You would have been only a kid, Dido.

DIDO: There were no kids after Bloody Sunday.

HARK: Only the dead and the dying.

PAUL: Can you remember their names?

HARK: The dying or the dead?

PAUL: Bernard McGuigan, forty-one years, Inishcairn Gardens, Derry.

GRETA: The smell of death on the streets of Derry, I find it still.

PAUL: Patrick Doherty, thirty years, Hamilton Street, Derry.

HARK: Lie down and die or fight.

PAUL: Michael Kelly, seventeen, from Dunmore Gardens, Derry.

HARK: I tried to fight.

PAUL: William McKinney, twenty-seven, from Westway, Derry.

HARK: Or did I die?

PAUL: James Wray, twenty-three, Drumcliffe Avenue, in Derry.

SEPH: We all died.

PAUL: Hugh Gilmore, seventeen years old, Garvan Place, Derry.

HARK: I didn't die.

PAUL: Jack Duddy, who was seventeen, Central Drive, Derry.

SEPH: In a way we all died.

PAUL: William Nash, nineteen, Dunree Gardens, Derry. Michael McDaid, twenty-one, Tyrconnell Street, Derry. Gerald Donaghy, seventeen, Meenan Square, Derry. John Young, seventeen, Westway, Derry.

GRETA: Were they that young?

PAUL: Kevin McElinney, seventeen, Philip Street, Derry.

GRETA: Were they all that young?

PAUL: Gerald McKinney, Knockdara House, Waterside, Derry.

GRETA: Were we all that young?
(*Silence.*)
MAELA: When I was young, at school like, I quite liked poetry.
GRETA: What put that into your head?
MAELA: Poetry? The names of the dead. I don't remember any poems. I tell a lie. I do remember one. How did it go? ' "Is there anybody there?" – '
PAUL: 'said the Traveller,
    Knocking on the moonlit door.'
MAELA: 'The Traveller', that's it.
PAUL: No, it's called 'The Listeners'.
SEPH: I learned that as well.
HARK: Beat into me.
DIDO: Same here.
GRETA: Did we all learn it?
SEPH: Yes.
GRETA: Say it.
PAUL: 'Is there anybody there?' said the Traveller,
    Knocking on the moonlit door.
GRETA: And his horse in the silence champed the grasses
    Of the forest's ferny floor.
    And a bird – and a bird –
SARAH: – a bird flew up out of the turret,
    Above the Traveller's head:
    And he smote on the door a second time;
    "Is there anybody there?" he said.
HARK: But no one descended to the Traveller;
    No head from the leaf-fringed sill
    Leaned over and looked into his grey eyes –
SEPH: Where he stood –
DIDO: – perplexed –
PAUL: – and still.
GRETA: But only a host of phantom listeners
    That dwelt in the lone house then
    Stood listening in the quiet of moonlight
    To that voice from the world of men . . .
SEPH: And he felt in his heart their strangeness –

PAUL: Their stillness answering his cry . . .
      For he suddenly smote on the door, even
         Louder, and lifted his head.

SARAH: 'Tell them I came, and no one answered,
         That I kept my word,' he said.

MAELA: Never the least stir made the listeners,
         Though every word he spake –

GRETA: Fell echoing through the shadowiness of the still house
      From the one man left awake.

WOMEN: Aye, they heard his foot on the stirrup,
         And the sound of iron on stone
      And how the silence surged softly backward,
         When the plunging hoofs were gone.

    (*Silence.*)

GRETA: What time is it?

MAELA: To wash the dead.

    (MAELA *suddenly spreads one of the white sheets on the
    ground.*)

PAUL: Is it after twelve?

MAELA: Sunday.

GRETA: Sunday.

SARAH: Sunday.

    (*The women start to place the guns, balaclavas and religious
    images on to the sheet.*)

GRETA: Wash the dead.

PAUL: Sunday.

MAELA: Bury the dead.

SEPH: Sunday.

SARAH: Raise the dead.

HARK: Sunday.

DIDO: Do you see the dead?

GRETA: The dead beside you.

SEPH: Sunday.

MAELA: The dead behind you.

PAUL: Sunday.

SARAH: The dead before you.

SEPH: Change.

PAUL: Changed.
HARK: Forgive the dead.
MAELA: Forgive the dying.
SARAH: Forgive the living.
GRETA: Forgive yourself.
MAELA: Forgive the earth.
SARAH: Forgive the sun.
GRETA: Forgive the moon.
HARK: Forgive yourself.
MAELA: Bury the dead.
GRETA: Raise the dying.
SARAH: Wash the living.

(*Light begins to break through the graveyard's standing stones. At first its beam is narrow, golden and strange, like a meeting of the sun and moon. Birdsong begins. The light increases in power, illuminating them all. The birdsong builds to a crescendo. Looking at each other, they listen, in their light.*)

SCENE NINE

Sunday morning. DIDO *stands in the graveyard. The others sleep.*

DIDO: What happened? Everything happened, nothing
happened, whatever you want to believe, I suppose.
(*Silence.*)
What do I believe? Well, I believe it is time to leave Derry.
Love it and leave it. Now or never.
(*Silence.*)
Why am I talking to myself in a graveyard? Because
everyone in Derry talks to themselves. Everybody in the
world talks to themselves. What's the world? Shipquay
Street and Ferryquay Street and Rosville Street and
William Street and the Strand and Great James Street.
While I walk the earth, I walk through you, the streets of
Derry. If I meet one who knows you and they ask, 'How's
Dido?' Surviving. How's Derry? Surviving. Surviving.
Carthage has not been destroyed. Watch yourself.
(*From his scrapbook* DIDO *tears flowers and drops them on the
sleepers.*)
Watch yourself, Hark and Sarah. Watch yourself, Greta.
Watch yourself, Paul and Seph. Watch yourself, Maela.
Remember me. Watch yourself, Dido. Watch yourself,
Derry. Watch yourself. Watch yourself. Watch yourself.
(DIDO *lets the scrapbook fall. It hits Seph's battered guitar,
still wrapped in the tricolour.* DIDO *lifts the guitar, half
unwrapping the tricolour. He places it on the sheets. He collects
the pile together and places it on the pyramid.*)
Play.
(DIDO *exits. Music begins, Mendelssohn, 'Song without
Words', Op. 19 No. 6. They sleep in the graveyard.*)

BAGLADY

Baglady was first performed at the Peacock Theatre, Dublin, in March 1985.

BAGLADY: Maurean Toal
Director: Patrick Mason
Designer: Frank Hallinan Flood

For Eoin and Maurean

The BAGLADY *wears the heavy clothes of a farmer, rough trousers, dark overcoat, boots. She is feminized only by a grey scarf protecting her head, hiding her hair completely. On her back she carries a grey, woollen sack. The* BAGLADY *walks along the edge of her space.*

BAGLADY: I saw someone drown once. I was carrying them in my arms. When I looked behind me, there was nobody there. I'm walking to the water. This place is full of it. The river's everywhere you look about you. Here's the very edge. I want to put something into it. If you take one step too close, you fall in. I saw someone drown. I saw. But I didn't tell. Tell me now. Tell me to the water that took you. Throw it in for what it's worth.

The BAGLADY *sings as she continues walking.*

Who's at the window, who?
Who's at the window, who?
A bad, bad man with a bag on his back
Coming to take you away.
Who's at the window, who?
Who's at the window, who?
Go away, bad man, with the bag on your back,
You won't take me with you today.

The BAGLADY *stops.*

Go away from me. Don't look at me. Don't come near. I'm not dirty. Do you hear? Go away. I'll tell my father what you call me. He's a respected man in these parts. A decent man. He'll nail you for the stories you tell about me. He hears you. He hears everything. Go away.

The BAGLADY *walks.*

I had a dream. I went to sleep. Nice and warm. I was all
blood. My mother cleaned me up. The white interlock
went red. When you're clean, that way they can't smell
you. They won't follow you. Nobody finds you. Just
yourself alone.

The BAGLADY *stands.*

When you're on your own, you know everything. You can
go anywhere. Look at me. I know this place like the back
of my hand. (*Holds out her palms.*) See these? I walk on
them. I call one home and the other here. That way you
can't get lost. Watch when your two hands meet. Like this.
That's a bridge where I stand watching the river beneath
me and the people about me crossing the bridge on their
business. Now I separate my hands. The bridge goes away,
but the place goes on. It doesn't have a name for it's
written on my hand, and your fingers can't talk. (*Holds up
her ten fingers.*) I carry places with me. These are all streets.
I walk through them every day on the way to the river.
They're full of people too, but I wouldn't look at them. I
just carry them with me. They're my mark. They'll be
buried with me. My father is buried. Dead and buried. I
carry him as well, here on my back. Every stitch behind
and before me, it belonged to him. Whatever I didn't need,
I buried with him. A good-living man, he worked hard for
what he got in this life. He never touched me, never raised
his hand, never. I haven't a bad word to say against him.
He played cards but he deserved respect. Respect his
grave. This is it. Don't touch my father, don't walk on his
grave. Walk on a grave, you desecrate it. You turn into a
thief. Thief! I saw you. I saw.

The BAGLADY *walks.*

Be careful where you walk these days. Everywhere's

74

dangerous. Full of corners you wouldn't know what's hiding behind. Lock your doors. Lock your windows at night always. Lock yourself up. If you keep walking, nobody follows you here or home. They might watch you but they won't follow you. I heed none of them. I walk on regardless. Let them look. I want nobody. I live on the bridge. I look down into the river. I saw somebody drown. I was carrying him in my arms, he started to cry because I was leaving our house with him. When was that? I don't remember. I remember before leaving I was bleeding, but where was it coming from? I can't remember. I remember our house full of people. They were talking with their mouths and teeth, and I saw my father's tongue. He was laughing one evening. He won the cards. My father was a good man. Not one of you are fit to tie his shoes. Not one of you. Don't dare tell me otherwise. My father was a gentleman. I give him my blessing. Our house was white, it had black windows at night-time and the door was red. It was never closed. We were an open house. Tramps of the day stood in a line outside our house, looking in at me and my father and my mother. One man had a fit. He was like a dog, a big, black dog. He had water coming from his mouth. Burntoes or Crumlish, that was his name. They were tinkers. They begged money. I remember big slices of toasted bread in their hands, butter running from it like blood from a cut. Burntoes, he was lame. He walked on a crutch. It had the shape of a man with a big head. My mother said to me that Burntoes was lame because one night he got drunk and because he had no house to live in he walked the streets. One night he met the devil. It was so cold that Burntoes let the devil lay hands on him. Burntoes felt the devil's touch haul him down to hell. When he put one foot into the devil's fire, Burntoes jumped that hard to get out of hell, he left part of his foot behind to burn. That's why he limped. That's why when he saw you at night he cut the sign of the cross on himself, in case you were the devil. In the name of the father. And of the son.

My father was not the devil. (*Beat.*) They slept in our byre.
They had the smell of cattle. Straw all over their clothes.
When they got drunk, Crumlish beat the life out of poor
Burntoes. Crumlish was a bad brute, but Burntoes never
left him. Nobody could separate them. When Burntoes
died, Crumlish squealed like a pig. He sounded like a
woman. They were like a married couple my mother said.

The BAGLADY *stops walking.*

My mother was married. She was a married woman. My
father and my mother lived in our house. It was white with
a red door, and there were black windows everywhere.
Even the door had a window. The windows were cut from
glass. Sometimes you could look into the window and see
your face. It moved, not like your face in the river
swallowing you for ever. You could take your face out of
the window. I looked through my face one day in the
window and I saw my father and my mother. My mother
wasn't there, and my father was moving. He called me by
my name. It was my mother's. My mother. My mother told
fortunes. She could read people's cards. Their faces told
her stories.

The BAGLADY *walks.*

I can walk for miles without limping. I never stop. See my
hands, they make a bridge when I link them. Beneath the
link there's water running. I stand on the bridge and look
over. I see. I saw the river. It flowed beside our house.
When I stood beside the river, our house looked a long way
away. That's where I lived then, in our house, and my son
lived in the river. Sit down, I'll tell you about the house.

From her coat pocket the BAGLADY *takes a slice of bread and a
bottle of red lemonade. She sits, eating and drinking.*

We had electric in the house. Different colours in every

room. I liked red the best. The same colour as this
lemonade. No, red's never the same, no matter what way
you look at it or see where you see it. When you look into
the sun, the red blinds you. Blood can do that too, if you cut
your head badly. The electric light's a different red again. It
was never black when you put the red light on. You could
see out through the windows even in the night-time. And
you could see in. I used to breathe on the glass and write my
mother's name and my father's name on it. In the morning
it was never there, the names. The sun wiped them out. It
was red too. But you can't drink the sun nor blood nor the
electric. This is all I touch, red lemonade. All I eat, white
bread. I like the colours of them. You need money to buy
the colours. My father had money. Wads of it lying on the
table or smelling in his hands. Sometimes there was a
picture of a woman in his smell. She looked like a mad
woman, dressed all strangely, all in green. A green lady. I
held her once in my hands the only time I was trusted with
money, because money's a man's responsibility. When you
get married, make sure it's to a man who knows the value
of money. If you don't, and you have money, give it away.
Give it away because money is a man's thing. Watch the
way money moves to a man's hand. Pound notes, fivers,
tenners, down on the table. I don't want it. It smells. Take
it away from me. Keep away from me. I'll tell on you, I'll
tell. We had electric in our house. It lit the whole room. I
could see everything. I could see the money. I don't want
it. Don't put out the light. Don't leave me in the black
room. If I can't see, I can't talk, and if I can't talk, I can't
tell. And I'm going to tell, I'm going to tell.

The BAGLADY *buries her face in her hands, then speaks to her
hands.*

My father gave me money. Where is it? What did I do with
it? Have I lost it? Where would I have spent it? Should I
throw it into the river? How was it got rid of? Answer me.

You know. You were there. Have you got a tongue between you? Have you lost that as well? I'll tear you apart. I'll cut your tongue out, if you don't tell me what happened to me. Tell me everything. Tell. Clap if you're going to tell me. Clap. Clap.

The BAGLADY *claps her hands.*

You were walking towards water. You were carrying something in these hands. We tried to tell you not to. You couldn't hear what you were carrying. Your Father was with you. He thought you were carrying him. So he took himself from your arms and he walked into the river, turning into a black dog, shaking the water from his hair. You held us out to him, but he wouldn't stop. Do you remember? Can we stop telling you now?

The handclapping stops. The BAGLADY *rises suddenly.*

Get away from me. Get away. Take that dog away. I hate dogs. It's a killer. It jumps on you and eats you up. Take it away. Red. Red. Out of my sight. Foot. Hand. Moving in the river. Don't bring it any nearer me. Chase it far away. Stomach. Blood. Neck. It doesn't move any more. It's gone away. Say the dog's gone away. Stop him following me. I'll shoot it dead. I'll drown the bastard. Give me peace. I deserve peace. I don't care what happened, just give me peace. Get this out of my sight.

The BAGLADY *tears the bread into bits and throws it about her.*

Melt.

The BAGLADY *sits.*

When things are torn, you can't put them back again. When something's taken from you, you can't get it back.

You can try, but what use? Look, do you see that dog who keeps following me, what do you think he's after? Wanting to be fed? I've nothing for him. He knows, but will he go away? No. What then does he want? Does he want me to tell him something? Or is he telling me? Are you asking or telling? Are you looking for this?

The BAGLADY *takes from her pocket a deck of playing cards. She kneels. The* BAGLADY *holds up the king of diamonds.*

Here is your beginning. It is always a sign of water. No matter what card is drawn, it says the same always. Why do you back away from it? Do you fear water? Do you fear birth? Do you fear it more than death? Or did someone die in troubled water? Your hand's shaking. Are you trying to catch them?

The card drops from the BAGLADY's *hand.*

Did you hear that falling? Was it a crack? It could have been your heart, it could have been your mind. Still, the sound was breaking, like a glass on the ground. Can you see into it? Tell me who's there, watching out? Do you see yourself? I see a man's reflection. He looks like yourself. It could be your father. Wait. There's another with him, standing by him. It's another man. A man younger than yourself. Could it be father and son? I might be wrong but they share a resemblance. They share a name. A family name. You have no name. You are not married. You have no family. Could these men be brothers? If so, are they friends now? Why is one of them drenched? Is he crying? Is the other dead? But which is doing the crying? Watch yourself beside water.

The BAGLADY *holds up another card.*

The five of clubs. A bad card. Don't worry, it's over. It's

youth. But it stands for suffering, because it means sorrow. Five black wounds of sorrow. They're healing since they're black, but you have something to confess. It happened long ago. Somebody did something and you did. Did whoever it was tell you to say nothing, or did you imagine their voice as your own? When you tried to tell eventually did nobody believe you, so you stopped believing too although you saw it all happening?

She places the card down.

Maybe your cards will tell you it wasn't your fault. You'll forgive. You'll forget. We all do. Forget, that is. That's what living's about. Forgetting. I believe you. I forgive you.

The BAGLADY *raises the queen of hearts.*

This is the queen of hearts. She comes without king or jack. Alone, this is a lucky card, for it shows you have a good heart, a woman's heart. She asks questions you'd never expect. She knows there is something hidden in your heart, a secret she could guess at, but she won't. All she'll say is that she too had a son. He was taken. The queen left her country in disguise as a beggarman, searching for her son. Every time she came to the place where she might find him all she found instead was the same answer. Your son is dead, his father killed him. She couldn't say my son is my father and my father is my son. She could not say it, but that was all she possessed, the truth. She wants you to receive. She knows you. Look. See who comes after.

The BAGLADY *raises the queen of spades.*

A black lady. Bitter. The quiet card. This one keeps her counsel because she's angry, and no one knows that anger's source. She has the face of a corpse. Is she woman at all?

There's some that doubt it. Does she remind you of anybody? Do you remember the queen of hearts? She had a son. Did he look like this? Is that why his father killed him? Do you see this one's cheek? There's a track across it. It could be the track of a fist. This woman's received a blow that will shut her up for ever, but she's with you through all your life.

The BAGLADY *shows the seven of diamonds.*

A seven for good luck, and here it's diamonds. That's for marriage. I know who's next to arrive. A man in black.

The BAGLADY *holds up the knave of clubs.*

You see, I thought there'd be a priest involved. When he asks you to do something, you can't say no. It might be at a funeral you met him, or else a wedding; there's very little difference between them, weddings and funerals, because they're all tied in some way to money. Let me see which is which here.

The BAGLADY *looks at the ace of spades.*

Oh Christ, I see death. You'll be attending a funeral. A young woman or a child's funeral. It's definitely somebody young. Don't panic. Taking all the cards together, I'd say there's good news in them. I shouldn't have mentioned death. But I saw it. What I see I have to tell. I have to say it.

The BAGLADY *starts to spread the cards in patterns on the ground.*

I knew a man once, God rest him. (*Lifts one of the seven cards.*) This is him here.

As the BAGLADY *tells his story, she manipulates the cards as characters.*

You'd think he had everything. He ruled the roost in his house. His wife and child walked in fear of his body and its strength. He had that much strength he wanted more. He wanted his wife's, he wanted his child's. Some nights he turned into a black dog and took himself out walking. Walked for miles, walked the feet off himself, walked himself into his grave. When this man died, the dog lived on. It went mad with grief. It knew who was master and one day this dog grabbed the man's daughter by the throat. She went hysterical but the dog wouldn't let go. It chained her up. Then one night the dog changed back to the man. When he spoke to his daughter she thought he was the devil. He said she was his wife. He'd come back for her. She got such a shock she jumped that hard from her chain that she tore her head away from the rest of her and all that was left behind was her skin and bones. The man whistled for his dog and it came running. He set the dog on his daughter's body and it ate all that was left of her. (*Beat.*) The first man I saw standing in the cards, the man beside water, the man at your beginning, the man with a family, I know now for sure that's my father.

The BAGLADY *rapidly gathers the cards together, returning them to the deck, shuffling it rapidly.*

I see the five of clubs. I see the queen of hearts, she knows the queen of spades. I see a man in black. That man is not your father, but you must call him father. The queen of spades starts smiling. She thinks she is your father. The five of clubs is love, but it will bring you sorrow. You will love your son but you must love your father. In the name of. In the name of. Jesus, he's dead. My father is dead.

The BAGLADY *howls. From her sack she hauls an iron chain. She beats it violently on the ground around her.*

Get out of my way. Do you not hear me? I'll knock you out
of my road with this boy if you don't move. This is what
I'm cut from. This is my fist. It will teach you respect for
what I say to you. Watch where I'm going. I'm on my way
to a wedding. This is my dress. It cost a fortune. Do you
hear that? This is all I own, so I value it. It was left to me
in a will. It was left by respectable people. A good man. A
good woman. I gave the world a good child.

The BAGLADY *sings:*

Who's at the window, who?
Who's at the window, who?

The BAGLADY *gathers the chain into her arms.*

It's yours. Take a good look at him. That's him in front of
you. Yours as much as mine. He's come to see you. Hold
him. He's yours. (*Drops the chain.*) That's my body. That's
your mother's body. Your mother's dead as well. (*Fingers
the ring of the chain.*) In our house there's a room made
from windows. I'm not allowed in, even to see out of it.
But I can see it clearly. That's where they sleep, my mother
and father. The room only appears when they're lying in it.
They can change the shape of our whole house. They have
magic. Sometimes my mother is my father and my father is
my father too. Sometimes they turn me into each other
when they think I don't know what they're doing but I do.
I always do. I watch them. I see them through the window.
I stand in the yard with the cattle and the dog on the chain.
I know what they've done. I saw through the window. But
I won't tell what I see, because it's a secret. I promised
myself.

The BAGLADY *tries to snap the chain in two.*

Tell me my name. Do I have a name? Is it a girl's name? Is

it a good name, a clean one? I wash my name like myself every morning. I wash my face and my neck. I wash my breast and my woman. I wash my legs. My feet. When I touch myself, I'm clean. I'm not afraid of drowning in a basin of water. If you don't go near water, you get dirty. Black as your boot. Black as your baby. In the water. My name is my father's. I lost it after him. He washed it away. I saw it all. I jumped through the window. It cut me in two. My father pulled me. I was all dirty. I roared out. I knew what happened to dirty girls. He knew. Dirty, dirty. Get away from the water. Don't leave me under it. I can't breathe. Let me go. My neck, it's sore. Your fist's like a knife. It's cutting me. I can't breathe. The water will rise and take me. I can't run away. I'm sore. I won't tell. I won't open my mouth. Let me go. I'll stay quiet. I'll be good. Let me out. I'm soaking. I'll turn into water. Let me go.

The BAGLADY *howls. She grows silent. She starts to rock her whole body gently.*

Ssssh, ssssh. Stop that crying. Hear me? Stop it. Be a good girl. Your daddy does it for your own good. You can be a bad girl. You have to do as your daddy tells you. Don't you? Stop that crying. Stop. Look at this. Look. (*Takes a ring from her pocket.*) Isn't this lovely? See the way it shines, even at night? You've never seen this before, have you? It's a ring, a ring for a wedding. That's for you. I gave it to your mother. It's gold, like your hair. When you grow up and get married, I'll buy you a wedding ring too. And a long white dress. And a big white cake. And lemonade to drink, red lemonade. You'll be crying when your daddy gives you away at the altar. Take the ring. See if it fits you. Does it fit? Good. You can keep it. Put it around your finger. They say if a girl sleeps with a wedding ring in her bed she will have lovely dreams about the man she'll marry, the house they'll have and all their children, boys and girls. Boys and girls together. Do you ever dream, Daddy? Do I ever dream? Will I tell you about my dream? It's about a good girl. She did as she was told. And she could keep a secret. A big secret. And because she could keep secrets, her father gave her a golden necklace. He trusted her with his life. When she kept her mouth closed, the necklace shone like the sun and she was beautiful, very beautiful. But if she breathed a word of their secrets, the necklace grew black, blacker and blacker, and it tightened about her throat, tighter and tighter, twisting her face up, so that she hardly had a face and she couldn't breathe again until she said she was sorry. Are you sorry? Are you a good girl? Are you? Are you?

The BAGLADY *holds out her arms. She embraces the air. Her embrace turns into a grasp. Her hands start to beat against her body. She fights her hands away. They reach for the chain. She curbs it with her foot. Her hands free the chain and raise it to her neck. It starts to coil itself tightly about her. She bites her hand as it coils the chain. It starts to uncoil. She holds the chain in her lap.*

Was it dead or was it alive? Was it a boy or a girl? How can you tell if it were alive or dead? Did you hear it breathing? Did it cry out? Did it have a name? Can I give it a name? Can I give it a kiss? A big kiss? A big kiss for Ma? A kiss for Daddy too?

Lifting the chain from her lap, the BAGLADY *winds it into a heap before her. She gathers up the scattered cards as she sings.*

Who's at the window, who?
Who's at the window, who?
A bad, bad man with a bag on his back
Coming to take you away.
Who's at the window, who?
Who's at the window, who?

Go away, bad man, with the bag on your back,
You won't take me with you today.

The BAGLADY *raises the the queen of hearts, questioning
it.*

Mother?

The BAGLADY *drops this card on to the heap of chain. She raises
the king of diamonds.*

Father?

The card drops on to the chain. The BAGLADY *raises the queen of
spades.*

Daughter?

The card drops on to the chain. The BAGLADY *raises the ace of
spades.*

Son?

The BAGLADY *tears the card in pieces. She drops the pieces into the
red lemonade bottle. She shakes the mixture. She pours the
contents on to the chain.*

Son.

The BAGLADY *places the bottle on top of the chain. She shuffles the
remainder of the cards.*

The BAGLADY *leaves the cards on the heap of objects.*

They're dead now, dead and buried. I buried them. I
married them.

BAGLADY

The BAGLADY *removes her scarf, showing her hair. She places the scarf on the pile of objects. The* BAGLADY *takes a white dress from her sack and holds it against her.*

A man visited her once. He said I am your father. He held her, his daughter, in his arms, his two arms. She couldn't move away or near to him. He gave her a kiss. His mouth cut her tongue like glass. She was all torn. She cried for a drink of water. She wanted to wash herself, to wash the dirty girl she was. But she stayed a dirty girl for ever. Face. Neck. All red for ever. Breast and woman. Pouring. Legs. Wet. Feet. She called on God to take her out of her father's house. A man in black came to the house and said she was a liar. But he forgave because he took her with him to the house of God. Women in black washed her. In fire, not water. They nailed her son to a river. When the water graved him, she heard her father crying. To please her father the woman died as well. They wouldn't bury her, she had to bury herself. She got up and walked into her coffin. But she saw. I saw. God forgive me, I saw.

The BAGLADY *takes the dress from her, dropping it into the heap. The* BAGLADY *takes the ring from her finger. She raises it to look at in the light.*

With this ring, I thee wed. This gold and silver, I thee give. With my body, I thee worship. And with all my worldly goods, I thee endow. In the name of the Father and of the Son and of the Holy Ghost.

The BAGLADY *drops the ring.*

Drown.